# THREE, FOUR ...
# BETTER LOCK
# YOUR DOOR

(Rebekka Franck, Book 2)

## WILLOW ROSE

Copyright Willow Rose 2016
Published by BUOY MEDIA LLC
All rights reserved.

No part of this book may be reproduced, scanned, or distributed in any printed or electronic form without permission from the author.

This is a work of fiction. Any resemblance of characters to actual persons, living or dead is purely coincidental. The Author holds exclusive rights to this work. Unauthorized duplication is prohibited.

Cover design by Juan Villar Padron,
https://juanjjpadron.wixsite.com/juanpadron

Special thanks to my editor Janell Parque
http://janellparque.blogspot.com/

**To be the first to hear about new releases and bargains from Willow Rose. Sign up to be on the VIP list below.**
 I promise not to share your email with anyone else, and I won't clutter your inbox.

- SIGN UP TO BE ON THE VIP LIST HERE:
http://readerlinks.com/l/415254

**Tired of too many emails?** Text the word: "willowrose" to 31996 to sign up to Willow's VIP text List to get a text alert with news about New Releases, Giveaways, Bargains and Free books from Willow.

FOLLOW WILLOW ROSE ON BOOKBUB:
https://www.bookbub.com/authors/willow-rose

# Prologue

THEY WERE HAVING SEX. RIGHT THERE ON THE BED IN FRONT OF HER. Well, they didn't know that she was there, did they? They didn't know that she was watching them. They didn't know that she had been watching them all night.

She was there when they met in the restaurant at the inn. She was watching him as he waited for her. She saw him smile and get up when the woman approached the table. She observed as they first shook hands then hugged each other awkwardly as people who have never met before often do. The woman was much older than he, she noticed. Ten, maybe fifteen years older. They were quite the pair, she thought to herself.

He ordered shrimp as an appetizer and roasted pork with parsley sauce and potatoes while she had salmon for appetizer then the Boeuf Béarnaise that the inn was so famous for.

In the soft light of the restaurant that hid the growing lines in her face she looked delicate with her dark hair and blue eyes. The man seemed to be struck by her beauty as well and had eyes for no one else during the dinner and subtle conversation.

They talked about the weather, the Indian summer that the small kingdom of Denmark was experiencing this September. Usually the summer was long gone by now and the fall with its strong winds and cold had taken over. But not this year, the man said with a smile. This year the summer had been better than most years. Maybe global warming wasn't that bad after all, he said and they both laughed.

He had been charming. A true gentleman. He poured wine in her glass at just the right time, nodded and smiled politely looking like he was truly interested in listening to her stories. They both avoided talking much about themselves and neither was even sure that they knew the other party's real name. They had presented themselves as Troels and Anna, but both knew it wasn't uncommon in dates like these that one of the two involved - or even both of them - would give a false identity. After all they were never going to see each other again after this, so why bother with a true identity? Why risk the wife or husband discovering your secret escapades, dark desires that went unfulfilled in the sex lives of the married. After all the secrecy was for many the most thrilling part.

But even if they never told each other much, she knew about them. She knew their dirty secrets. Yes, the woman watching them from the other table knew more about both of them than they would ever reveal to each other. She thought about it when she giggled along while listening in on their growingly embarrassing conversation that soon became strained because they were running out of subjects to discuss.

They were holding hands across the table, letting their fingers rub against each other. The black haired woman who called herself Anna had laughed at Troels' words and thrown her head backwards in the delight of his company. It caused the woman watching to shiver with a combination of joy and utter disgust.

At one point Anna turned her head, perhaps perceiving the fixed stare coming from the woman sitting at the table next to them, seeking the cause of that uncomfortable sensation of being watched.

The music from the piano-player in the corner of the restaurant was perfect to set the mood, understated enough to make the two people want to get closer and leave the restaurant to go to the room they had rented just for the night. A night meant for pleasure - and pain.

The woman followed them up the stairs as Troels teased Anna and made her laugh while they walked towards the room feeling the thrill of what was about to happen.

The joy of expectation was always the biggest joy, the woman watching thought to herself. It was for them and it was for her.

It made it easier for her that they hadn't locked the door, she thought as she watched them during the act in the bed. She watched them in silence as they moved their sex-act to the bathroom where Troels tied up Anna with hand-cuffs and then entered her from behind. The woman watching through the frosted glass felt a thrill of excitement go through her body as Troels pulled the black hair and Anna screamed. The woman watching was almost aroused when Troels hit Anna and whipped her with his brown belt. Anna screamed at the top of her lungs. She screamed with what had to be pleasure and desire, since she never said the safe-word that the woman watching had heard them agree on during the dinner. Anna yelled that he should stop, she begged, she pleaded and called him master. But it only made him beat her even more while he rode her from behind. They were moaning, screaming and shouting nasty things to each other.

The woman watching had to restrain herself from getting off, from jumping in and joining them, from clapping and screaming out her own lust and desire.

It was after all supposed to be a surprise.

## Chapter 1

"I DON'T WANT TO DO GYMNASTICS ANYMORE," JULIE SAID WHILE staring out the window.

We were driving in my car. It was a Thursday morning like so many others. Except I had never heard Julie utter those words before. She had loved gymnastics up until now. She looked forward to them all week and when Thursday finally arrived she would find it hard to wait until school was over and she could go. She was really good at gymnastics. She was by far the best in her group, her teacher told me. So why this? I asked myself. Why now?

"What are you talking about? You love gymnastics!" I said and drove up in front of the school. I parked the car and turned off the engine. My eight-year-old Julie sighed deeply sounding horribly like a teenager. It was a little too early for that, I thought.

"I just don't want to do it anymore, okay?"

"Is this about your father again? I know you haven't seen him in two years but don't let his absence destroy everything you're fond of. I know it was his suggestion many years ago that you start gymnastics, but you've grown to love it so much. It would be a pity if you stopped doing it just because you want to punish your dad or something."

Julie sighed again. "Not everything I do has to do with dad not being here," she growled. "Jeez, Mom, you always think I'm so mad at him for leaving me, but I really am not." She turned her head and glanced at me.

"Then what is it? Is it me?" I asked.

She shrugged. "I just want to do other stuff, okay?"

"Like what?"

"I don't know."

"Julie. This is silly. You're so good at gymnastics. You used to love it so much." I put my hand on her arm. "Don't you think it's a little too hasty? Shouldn't we wait and see in a couple of weeks? Maybe you'll enjoy it again next week?"

She rolled her eyes. "It's just so ..."

"So what?"

"So childish."

"Well you're a child, so that should suit you fine then." I looked at my watch. "I'm running late, Sweetie. Let's talk about this later."

"Whatever."

I grabbed her arm just as she was about to get out of the car. "Julie. Did something happen? You know you can tell me if it did, right?"

She nodded. Then she left the car and I drove off. I was still wondering about her as I ran up the stairs towards Zeeland Times' editorial room in Karrebaeksminde. When had she turned into a teenager? I thought as I opened the door.

Sara barely noticed me enter the office. Staring at her computer-screen, she wore a headset to listen to the police-scanner. As always, she had an extra large coffee and was eating chocolate cake. She waved to me when she finally noticed my arrival.

"Morning," I growled, threw my bag at the desk and pulled out my laptop. I went into the kitchen for coffee and stared at the remains of the chocolate cake on the table. For a few seconds I considered just plunging in, digging my fingers into it and shoveling the gooey chocolate into my mouth. But of course I didn't. I was after all trying to lose those last five pounds that had become eight since I had Julie. Admittedly, I had gained a lot of weight ever since I moved back to my hometown. If it was my father's cooking and insisting on putting butter in everything or Sara's cake marathon during working hours that had done this to me, or because I stopped smoking, I didn't know. Maybe I didn't care anymore. Little by little I was getting used to the thought that maybe I wasn't going to get rid of it again. I was never going to be as slim as I had been before I had Julie. Maybe it was about time I just made peace with my thighs.

I sipped my coffee and decided to just have a small piece. It wasn't like I had anyone who was going to see me naked soon anyway. Swimsuit season was over for now even if we did have some late Indian summer right now, I wasn't about to go to the beach anyway. Plus fall would come any day now and then I would have another entire year to lose that piece of chocolate cake. I deserved it I thought and took a slightly bigger piece than planned.

Sara smiled at me when she saw my plate as I sat at my desk. Her chubby cheeks looked like she was hoarding food for later. I stared at my cake and wondered if I would eventually turn into her if I kept this up? Would I wear big tent-like dresses with flowers? Would I let my hair grow wild and try to tame it with a butterfly hairpiece? Would I waddle when I walked?

I had nothing against Sara, don't get me wrong, she was one of the nicest women I had met and I enjoyed working with her immensely even if she made a terrible mess at the office with her stacks of newspapers and magazines. I just wasn't sure I wanted to end up like her, chubby and living alone with her two dogs that were as fat as she was.

"How's everybody doing this morning?"

I lifted my head and smiled at Sune who had just entered the editorial room. He smiled back and came towards me. I swallowed the last bite of chocolate cake and waved at him.

"Chocolate today, huh?" He asked with a grin. His green Mohawk swayed as he moved his head. "Is it better than the carrot cake you had yesterday?"

"There's more in the kitchen if you want," I said with the remains of the cake still in my mouth.

"No thanks," he said and tapped his stomach. "Watching my weight."

"Oh come on," I exclaimed.

Sune was skinny and tall. Plus he was almost ten years younger than me so he could still eat anything. I on the other hand was getting closer to forty and knew those days of eating everything I wanted were over.

"Well, okay. Maybe just a small piece," he said.

"Help yourself."

Sune disappeared into the kitchen and came back with a much bigger piece than what I had just inhaled. The remorse was growing inside of me as I swallowed the last bite.

"So what are we up to today?" he asked with his mouth full.

"Budget negotiations at city hall," I said. "They came through last night. We just need some happy comments from the mayor and then some angry ones from the opposition. Piece of cake, really."

Sune smiled. "Sounds sexy."

"Depends on what turns you on," I said grinning.

"Well it's not politics. Especially not local politics like this."

I shrugged. "You'd be surprised to know how many people disagree with you."

"I'd be surprised if you could find me one single person who is turned on by this kind of stuff."

"What about the mayor himself?" I asked. "Don't you think Mrs. Mayor got a little extra treatment in bed last night after the negotiations?"

I got up from my chair and grabbed my jacket from behind my chair. I brought a pen and a notepad. It was an easy assignment so I expected to be back before lunch. That would give me a couple of hours to write the story and then I would be home with my family early in the afternoon. That was one of the benefits of working on a small newspaper like this. I got to spend much more time with my family and my daughter especially loved those days when I came home early. When I had been a star reporter for a big national newspaper I never had this kind of time. I barely ever made it home for dinner and on weekends there would always be something, some story that I just had to look into. It was another life now. It was calmer and more family-friendly. I kind of enjoyed it.

"I really wish you hadn't said that," Sune said and held the door for me. He had his camera around his neck. "Now I won't be able to look at the mayor without picturing him with his wife."

## Chapter 2

THERE WASN'T MUCH SUSANNE LARSEN HADN'T TRIED BEFORE sexually. She'd had numerous lovers and tried all kinds of positions and everything from bondage to S/M. She loved it all. The tougher the better. She loved role playing, whips, handcuffs, restraints and even blindfolds. She loved being beaten, the feeling of pain on her skin, the hair pulling and even biting. It all turned her on and always had.

Her husband of course knew nothing of her secret desires, nor was he ever going to. That was why Susanne always met up with strangers she found on a dating site on the Internet. A site only for people of her kind. Only for people who liked what she liked, and she liked it rough. This website made it easier for her to find a match, find someone who wanted to treat her the way she liked to be treated.

She started by writing to them once she found someone who matched her profile. After a couple of weeks flirting and writing dirty messages they would agree to meet. She loved the anonymity of it since she preferred to not know anything about the men she had sex with. That's also why she never agreed to meet more than once. She didn't want to risk feeling anything for them if she got to know them. They were supposed to be complete strangers who only wanted her for the sex. Who wanted to use her, exploit her vulnerability and penetrate her until she could take it no more. She liked to be treated like a whore and submit herself to the mercy of some handsome stranger in the dark whom she would never see again afterwards. She let them use her and she would scream her painful pleasure out all night.

Then she would go home to her family the very next day and be the wife and mom she was expected to be. That was the way she wanted it and that was how she lived.

She never thought much about her family while she was with the stranger, but for some inexplicable reason she did think of them that particular day. That day with the tall, dark, very young guy in the room at the inn in Karrebaeksminde. For just a few seconds she thought about her son and daughter at home in their beds and their father sitting alone in the living room watching some sports like he always did. She thought about them and felt for the first time a slight feeling of guilt and remorse that she couldn't escape. It was like a pinch in her heart.

Maybe it was because this one was handsomer than any of the others she had been with. Charming too. In fact he reminded her of one of the doctors at the hospital where she worked as a nurse, the one she'd had a huge crush on for months now. That had turned her on immediately once she saw him in the restaurant at the inn.

When he had told her that his name was Troels, she hadn't believed him, but decided to just play along. She had called herself Anna. It was her mother's name, but since she had died when Susanne was fourteen she was certain that she wouldn't mind. Served her right anyway for the way she had treated Susanne, she thought. Served her right for never interfering when her father climbed into Susanne's bed at night. Served her right for never stopping him and never listening to Susanne when she told her about it and asked her mother to make it stop.

Troels started off by slapping her across the face once they had entered the hotel room. He then kicked her in the back and threw her on the bed. She screamed but enjoyed it very much. The slapping around, the pulling of her hair was just like her father had done.

"Tell me I'm a little whore," she said. "Tell me what you'll do to me now."

"You little dirty whore," he said with a harsh voice.

Oh boy that turned her on. Those words really did it for her. Just like her father had always said when he climbed into her bed. "More, more," she begged.

"You dirty little slut. I am going to make you pay for all you've done. When I'm done with you, you won't be able to walk for two weeks. I am going to beat all those naughty things out of you. And then I'm going to use you. You'll be my toy, you'll be my slave."

"Oh yes, master. Use me. Make me your slave," she groaned.

Then he pulled her by the hair off the bed and into the bathroom where he pushed her against the shower door. That was a new one; she thought and smiled while he cuffed her hands. Then he hit her again. He entered her from behind with the scream of a wild beast before he beat her with his belt. She screamed in pain. Her secret lover told her he had more toys in his bag in the car and he was going to get them. He told her to stay put. Then he laughed as he left her in the shower. Beaten, broken, bleeding. Left to the mercy of a stranger.

This was what she wanted, she thought to herself while waiting for his return, wondering with a shiver what kind of toys he had brought. This was what she longed for but could never get with her husband who thought she was nothing but an ordinary woman, wife, mother and nurse. She could never share this with him. She could never tell him her dirty little secret, could she?

She didn't finish the thought before the frosted door to the shower opened and a face was revealed. Panic arose inside of her as she stared into the eyes of a woman in a long blue dress. Frantically she pulled her hands but they remained stuck in the handcuffs. The woman in the elegant blue evening dress smiled and stared at her with wild manic eyes that seemed to enjoy the fear in hers. She lifted her hand and showed a small scalpel much like the ones doctors at the hospital used.

Yes, Susanne Larsen had tried almost everything sexually over the last many years living her secret double-life, but she could say for certain that she had never done this.

## Chapter 3

Kenneth Juhlersen was having a bad day.

He lost his job during the recession and then started a cleaning business on his own, working hard the last three years. He built it all up so he and his wife would have a decent retirement, something to look forward to, travel a little, and see the world.

Being fired was the worst thing to ever happen to him at the time. It had almost destroyed him. He was so close to retirement. Who would hire a car salesman who was almost sixty years old and whose biggest accomplishment was selling seven Toyotas on the same day once back in the early nineties? They had named him "The brave tailor" since he had struck seven in one day like the little tailor in the fairy-tale who had killed seven flies. They removed the "little" since Kenneth was big like a Viking and calling him "the brave little tailor" would just be strange. But what good did that do him when he was fired due to cut-backs? All he had left after twenty-five years selling cars was his nickname. What was he supposed to do two years before his retirement?

At the same time his wife Bettina was constantly bothering him about the winter garden that she had wanted for ten years, which he had once promised her. Being a man of his word he wanted to keep his promise to her. That was when he decided to take fate into his own hand. He grabbed his wife's cleaning equipment, the bucket, the mop, the vacuum cleaner and put it all in the back of the car. Then he started going door to door asking if anyone needed his service. At first his wife was terrified since he had been all over their own neighborhood and she did not care for the neighbors to know that her husband had to stoop this low. But once the money started coming in she suddenly saw the possibility of finally getting her winter garden and they had agreed that Kenneth Juhlersen was allowed to go door to door in any neighborhood other than their own.

Today, three years later, he had three employees working for him. The order with the local inn was one he recently landed so it was of the utmost importance that nothing went wrong. It was the order that could finally put him over the top. If he kept this client satisfied he didn't have to take others any longer. He no longer had to clean people's houses, and Bettina would get her winter garden.

So when they had called from the inn this same morning and told him that his employee Annette hadn't shown up Kenneth Juhlersen knew had to go himself. It was like he had always said: if you want something done right you have to do it yourself.

Kenneth Juhlersen had cleaned four rooms by nine thirty and now he walked down the hallway pushing his wagon. He stopped in front of a door and pulled out the key from his pocket. It was an old inn and they had kept the old-fashioned keys instead of replacing them with the key-card system that so many hotels used these days. This place was different. They wanted to keep everything in that old style making people think they had found a piece of the old fashioned Denmark that was charming and romantic. Kenneth Juhlersen knocked first like he had trained his employees to always do.

"Cleaning-service."

No one answered. Since there was no "do not disturb" sign on the door he put the key in the door. That was when he realized that it was already open.

"Hello? Cleaning service," he said again while slowly pushing the door open.

Still no answer.

Kenneth Juhlersen shrugged and entered by pushing his wagon through the old white-painted door with golden handles. He sighed and plugged in the vacuum cleaner. This was not how he had pictured his life at sixty-three. He was supposed to have retired by now and travel the world with his wife of nearly forty years. But fate had another opinion apparently. Not only had he lost his well-paid job at the Toyota dealer and lost his retirement bonus at fifty-nine, but last night he had also discovered that his wife in fact hadn't gone to Alanya in Turkey with her best friend Lisbeth for a 'girl's week out.' She was there with another man.

Kenneth Juhlersen pushed the vacuum cleaner across the carpet aggressively hitting table corners and chairs on the way. He thought about the night before when he was sitting in his living room watching the news when the phone rang. He picked it up and to his surprise talked to a woman he had never heard about before.

"My name is Lone Bendner," she said. "You don't know me, but I know you. I need to talk to you."

At first he had thought it was a wrong number or a clever phone sales trick. But it wasn't.

"I am calling you because I have information about your wife that I think you'd like to know. See she knows my husband Ole from work. They both work at TDC - the phone company. They met at a conference last year in Naksskov. They've been seeing each other since at hotels, telling us they were going to conferences and so on. I know this because I checked his e-mails today and found a bunch coming from your wife where they planned all this. If you know her e-mail and password maybe you can log in and see for yourself. I know this is probably a lot to take in, I know it was for me, but I thought you should know. I know I would want you to tell me if it was the other way around."

Kenneth Juhlersen gasped for air. His heart was beating fatally fast in his chest. His hands felt sweaty and couldn't hold on to the phone right. He was certain he was about to have another heart attack like the one he had three years ago just after he was fired. But it wasn't a heart attack. This was how it felt to be hit by reality. A reality so hard to comprehend that it made him feel sick.

"Hello. Mr. Juhlersen? Are you still there?" The voice of Lone Bendner sounded distant, as if it was coming from another world. The world where wives cheated on their husbands and lied to them about where they were.

"Are ... are you telling me that ..." Kenneth Juhlersen stuttered.

"Yes, Mr. Juhlersen. Your wife is with my husband in Alanya."

That was when he dropped the phone to the ground. He heard Lone Bendner's voice fade away while he walked towards the kitchen. In the cabinet above the fridge he grabbed the thirteen year old scotch that he had gotten as a farewell gift from the Toyota-dealer three years ago. He didn't even bother to find a glass. He just opened the bottle and started pouring the liquor into his mouth until he couldn't hear Lone Bendner's annoying voice anymore.

Kenneth Juhlersen turned off the vacuum cleaner and picked up a dress from the floor. He found a hanger and put it nicely in the closet. His head hurt like hell when he bent over. But the hangover wasn't the worst part. He was mad. Angry, almost furious. He would most definitely fire Annette after all this. No doubt about it.

"Not showing up for the most important client," he mumbled while picking up a stiletto from the floor and putting it in the corner of the room. "What do I care if she has three kids? If you don't show up you get fired. That's just the way it is."

Kenneth Juhlersen sighed when he found the other stiletto. He knew perfectly well he could never fire anyone. Nor could he stay mad long at his wife for cheating on him. Who could blame her? he thought, glancing at his reflection in the mirror across from the bed. He was bald and fat. Kenneth Juhlersen sighed again. He always thought that he could keep his wife happy if he made sure she had everything. Apparently that wasn't enough. He grabbed his bucket and put on his rubber gloves.

Kenneth Juhlersen was indeed having a very bad day and when he went into the bathroom of room 445 and saw the blood smeared on the frosted glass in the shower, he knew it was about to get much worse.

## Chapter 4

THE INTERVIEW WITH THE MAYOR WENT SMOOTHLY AS EXPECTED. He was happy naturally and the opposition wasn't. Sune took pictures while I interviewed them both at city hall and then we left. We bought Smoerrebroed on our way home, a Danish specialty, a kind of open sandwich on rye-bread that everybody eats for lunch.

Sara hadn't moved since we left. She was still sitting at her desk staring into the computer-screen when we entered the editorial room. She didn't react when I lifted the bag with the food and yelled "Lunch is here!"

That was when I knew that something was up. Sara was scribbling on a notepad next to her while listening intently to the scanner. I shrugged and looked at Sune. He went into the kitchen and brought out plates. Sara was still extremely focused while we ate.

"It's not like her to be that engrossed," Sune said. He plugged his camera into the computer and began uploading the pictures.

"You think it is important?" I asked.

It had been awhile since I last had a really big story to put in the papers. Actually come to think of it, it had been almost two years since Karrebaeksminde had been the scene of the first serial killer in Denmark. I was deeply involved in solving that mystery and earned a lot of credit from my editor. But since then I hadn't had any great stories, so I was feeling a little excited as I watched Sara jotting notes on her pad. Maybe this was finally something I could put in the paper; maybe this could be a cover story? Oh how I wished it was so. I needed it. I had felt so stuck lately. Karrebaeksminde was so drowsy I was afraid it was going to drag me down with it. I was after all still a reporter always on the lookout for a great story to tell.

Sara finally looked at me as she took off the headset.

"So what have you got for me?" I asked and wiped my mouth with a napkin. The taste of fish and remoulade sauce remained in my mouth. I drank some orange soda.

"Something is definitely going on," she said. "You have to move fast."

My eyes met with Sune's. He signaled that he was ready and hurried up eating the rest of his lunch. I leaned over my desk. "What is it?"

"I don't know but they've called all officers to report at Astrupgaard, the local inn just outside of town."

"What happened?" Sune asked.

"I don't know. They've called for backup from all police stations nearby. That's all I know."

I looked at Sara. "Do you think we should check it out? It doesn't sound like much of a story."

"I think it is. Something huge is going on down there. I received a call earlier from someone telling me that they had blocked the building with crime tape and just a minute ago I heard them calling for the forensic team from Copenhagen over the scanner," Sara said. "I think this might interest you."

I got up from my chair and grabbed my jacket. "That sounds like something worth checking out," I said and looked at Sune.

He swallowed the last bite of his lunch and grabbed his camera.

"We're out of here," I said to Sara. "Lunch is in the kitchen."

Astrupgaard Inn was one of those old-fashioned inns found in most small cities in Denmark. It was romantic and old and had very low ceilings since people were so much smaller back when it was built. It was very charming with its wooden floors and thatched roof. It was perfect for a romantic getaway or for the tourist who wanted to see some of small town Denmark and stay in a place that had good food.

Today however the tourists found it everything but charming, though. People had been asked to leave their rooms and stay in the lobby while the police searched the entire inn. One by one the guests were interrogated and reports were taken of their whereabouts the last twenty-four hours and if they had heard or saw anything suspicious around.

The atmosphere was intense when we arrived, to put it mildly. Through the windows I could see people sitting everywhere in the lobby, on the chairs, the table and even some on the floor. Some were talking amongst themselves, shaking their heads not knowing what was going on or wondering why their vacation was ruined like this. Some were crying, others laughing at the ridiculous situation, but common for everybody was that they couldn't go anywhere. They couldn't go back to their room and they couldn't leave the hotel. Police orders, they were told.

The police had blocked the entrance with crime-tape and two officers were standing by the entrance doors to keep anyone from leaving or entering.

"I'm sorry. You can't enter," the officer said to me as I tried to walk in. "There is an investigation going on and I cannot allow you to enter."

I showed him my press-badge. "Rebekka Franck, Zeeland Times," I said.

The officer sighed. Then he nodded and opened the door so we could walk in. "Okay. But stay in the lobby with the rest. We don't want to have anyone touching anything that might be important evidence."

"Could I talk to a spokesman from the police?"

"I'll make sure to find someone. But don't expect it to be quick. We're pretty busy as you can tell. All officers are working."

"Of course. Maybe you could tell me a little about what is going on?" I asked.

Sune started taking pictures of the lobby with all the people and the officers.

"I am afraid, I can't. I'll make sure to find someone who can," the officer said.

"Thanks."

I turned and looked at the many guests stuck in this small lobby. There was my story already, I thought to myself. Tourists trapped for hours while a crime was investigated by the police. I spotted an elderly woman sitting in a rococo chair. She was shaking her head in anger. Perfect I thought and approached her.

"Hello. Rebekka Franck, *Zeeland Times*," I said and held out my hand.

She looked at me a little perplexed.

"Now the media is here too?" she asked.

"Well I am. I'm from the local paper. Do you mind if I ask you some questions?"

The lady shook her head and her poodle hair moved along with it. "Do I look like I have anything else to do?"

I smiled. "Could you start by telling me what is going on? What have they told you?" I asked, turning to a blank page on my notepad.

"Nothing. Nothing is what they've told us. The police came banging at our door this morning when my husband and I were getting ready to leave for our trip to Gavnoe Castle and see the wonderful flower garden of tulips that I have been so looking forward to. They told us to walk down to the lobby without touching anything and without taking any of our possessions with us. Now all of my jewelry is in my bag up there and my husband's expensive watch and laptop and we don't know if we will see it all again. At first I thought 'Well this must be some kind of fire drill or something.' Now we have been here for almost three hours and still nothing. They haven't told us anything about what is going on or what they are looking for. There are rumors of course, but I don't know if any of that could be true."

"What kind of rumors?" I asked while my eye caught Sune's. I signaled that we needed pictures of the lady while she spoke. He approached quickly.

"Well some say that they had a bomb threat this morning, but wouldn't they have us outside the building instead of inside if that was the case?"

"I guess they would," I agreed.

"Others say that they're looking for some terrorist that is hiding at the inn. They're searching all the rooms to see if he is in there."

"That sounds plausible. It could be some criminal trying to hide from the police," I said and noted the rumor. No matter what it turned out to be it was a great story that they kept the guests uninformed for hours. Plus it had to be more than just a small time criminal since they went to so much trouble and pulled people out of their rooms. This would eventually hurt the inn's image and reputation of a quiet romantic place to spend a vacation. The owners couldn't be happy about that.

"Then I heard a third rumor that they've found someone dead in one of the rooms," the lady continued.

I stopped writing and looked at her. "A guest?" I asked.

"I don't know," she said with speculative eyes. "I guess. Maybe they think that one of us did it? Maybe they'll come down in a little while and point at someone and tell everybody why and how he did it?"

Maybe someone was watching too many crime-shows on TV, I thought chuckling to myself.

In the corner of my eye I spotted someone from the inn. He was talking to some of the guests and seemed to be trying to calm them down but that only made them madder. People were flocking around him asking questions, making demands for compensations, wanting to know exactly what was going on here. I felt so sorry for the poor guy. I wondered what bet he had lost to own the honor of being the first to show his face here. I hoped they had at least promised him a raise. I signaled Sune to take the guy's picture while he was surrounded by the angry crowd.

"I know it is a very difficult situation for our guests right now," I heard him say. But his words were drowned by the many angry voices.

"Now why can't we at least be allowed to go back to our rooms and get our things so we can leave this awful place," a woman said. Her voice was like a blowtorch cutting through wood.

"Yeah," someone replied. "We haven't done anything wrong. We are decent citizens we demand respect and decent treatment. We are all taxpayers. Is this what the government is spending our money on? Do we really deserve this after paying our taxes for twenty years without complaining?"

"I ... I really don't know," the inn employee stuttered. "I just work here. They haven't even told me what is going on. All I know is that we all need to stay right here until they are done with the investigation and I came here to tell you all that the inn offers you a complimentary dinner tonight at the restaurant free of charge, naturally."

I scoffed and shook my head while I noted it on my pad.

"A free dinner?" someone yelled from the crowd. They were getting ready to lynch the guy, I thought.

There was lots of murmuring and mumbling among the guests that eventually got louder and louder. Luckily for the employee a police officer of a higher rank appeared behind him. He lifted his hand to calm the crowd.

"Now if we could please just all settle down a little," he said and stepped up in front of the cornered guy from the inn.

"We would just like an explanation of what is going on," the woman with the blowtorch voice said.

"Of course you all do," the officer said. He was a handsome man of about fifty. He had a deep, authoritative voice that made everybody feel comfortable and safe in his presence. He was extremely trustworthy.

"The thing is that a crime has been committed at this hotel and we have to do our duty to our hard-working taxpaying citizens and find out who did it and put him away so he won't bother anyone again. That's our job. All we ask is for you to bear with us and show us some patience while we work. This inn has many rooms that need to be searched for evidence. That's why it is taking some time to complete. But it is necessary in order to find this criminal. Is that acceptable?"

The crowd had gone completely silent while he spoke. Someone nodded.

"Could we ask what kind of crime?" I asked.

The officer looked up into my eyes. "I see the press is here as well," he said with a forced smile. "Well I am very sorry, but I can't get into that yet," he said. "We will however have a press conference tomorrow for all members of the press."

"Should the guests at the inn be afraid?" I asked.

"I shouldn't think so," he replied. He was getting ready to leave.

## Three, Four ... Better lock your door

"But maybe you could tell us why you have called in the forensic team from Copenhagen?"

The smile on the officer's face stiffened. "I can't go into details right now," he said to the crowd. "But rest assured that we will catch this criminal. Just give us a couple of hours more and we will be done. Then you'll be able to return to your rooms again. I think we have taken a statement from all of you by now and we will be in touch if needed."

He pointed at me and signaled that I should follow him as he walked away. I grabbed Sune's arm and dragged him with me.

"Please don't scare people like that again," he said as we walked towards the stairs.

"I won't if you'll give me something to put in my paper," I said while Sune took pictures of us talking.

"What do you want?"

"I need details. What happened?" I asked.

The officer stopped and sighed. "I might as well tell you now. A woman was killed last night."

I froze and looked up from my pad. "Killed? How?"

"That I can't tell you. Not yet. We'll have to wait for the forensics report to state the exact cause of death."

"Was it murder? You could at least tell me that?"

He sighed again. "Yes."

"How can you be so certain?"

"Let's just say there is no doubt she was killed," he said.

"So what you're looking for in this hotel is a killer? That would be okay for me to write that?"

"Yes. Or evidence leading us to him."

"Anything so far?"

"No. And again ..."

"You can't tell me. I know."

"Has the family been informed yet?"

"Yes," he said heavily. "The victim's name is Susanne Larsen. She is from Naestved. She had a husband and two children. A son and a daughter, eight and eleven years old," he said.

I detected sadness in his voice. This case was really bad, I thought if it could shock an officer as experienced as him.

"Any descriptions, anyone you're looking for that I put in the paper? Any pictures of someone you need to talk to?"

He shook his head heavily.

"Nothing?"

"No," he repeated. "The room was booked in her name. She was seen having dinner with a man in the restaurant last night. We have found no trace of him anywhere in the room. No fingerprints, nothing. So naturally we are looking for him. He is described as tall, medium build and brown-haired."

"That's not much," I exclaimed. "So is it fair to say that the police are looking for a man who was seen having dinner with the deceased last night? Ask the public to bring in any information that they would think could lead to finding this guy?"

"That would be of great help, thank you."

"Well we have to help each other, right?" I said.

The officer nodded. "Now I need to get back," he said and started climbing the stairs. "I am afraid we still have a long way to go."

## Chapter 5

Back at the office I called my editor Jens-Ole at the headquarters. My hands felt sweaty and my heart was beating fast. It had been quite a while since I last had an exclusive story to present to him. I had a feeling that this could be a big one, one I would have to follow up on.

"I have a murder at the local inn. We're first with the story," I said.

"I'm listening," he answered.

"No other media was there. So it is ours exclusively," I repeated because I knew how important that was to an editor. That could make or break a story. If everybody else had it and had the same information it would be a small story in the back of the paper. But if it was our own we would make a big deal of it.

"Good, good, go on."

"A woman was found killed. They're certain it is a murder. No doubt about it they said. The guests at the inn were kept for hours in the lobby while they searched the place. We have interviews with guests and the police. Sune stayed behind to take more pictures and hopefully he will get one of the body leaving the place later today."

"That's great news," Jens-Ole said with enthusiasm.

That was one of the parts I really disliked about my job as a journalist. Someone's tragedy could be your happiness, your breakthrough, your exclusive. But that was just the way it was. You either learned to live with it or you couldn't be a journalist any longer. Editors like Jens-Ole loved murder stories especially if there were details and pictures.

"It's been a slow day today so you'll get the front page with this one," he continued. "Full page picture if you get the one of the victim leaving in a body bag."

"Wow," I said a little startled. I was going for a small note on the front page with a bigger article in the middle.

"I need you to write a small story for the online edition that will be published immediately while telling the readers more details will be in tomorrow's paper. Develop two larger big articles for the morning paper with more details. One about the killing for the front page and one about the frustrated guests at the inn on page three. Best spot in the paper. Happy?"

"Sure," I said.

"You should be. Get to work," he said and hung up.

I texted Sune: NEED PIX OF BODY LEAVING. CRUCIAL. STAY TILL YOU GET IT IF IT TAKES ALL DAY.

He texted back: 10-4.

Then I opened my laptop and started writing. The first one was about the woman who was murdered. I didn't have many details but what I had was enough to write a decent story. I sat back and reread the first draft once it was done. I was dissatisfied. What I had was all right but I wanted to know more. There were so many unanswered questions left and as an investigative reporter that didn't sit well with me. It was unsatisfying that I didn't even know how she had died. How was she killed? Was there a murder-weapon?

I looked at Sara who was still listening in on the police-scanner. Her eyes met mine and I signaled that she should take off the headset.

"Anything new?" I asked. "I've written the article and just want to be sure I have everything in it."

She shook her head. "They're all still at the inn."

"Okay. Thanks," I said.

Sara smiled and put her headset back on. I started writing the next article about the angry guests. This was more fun to write. I had several interviews with more angry guests after the officer left and their angry comments and demands made the article great. Less than two hours later I sent it all to Jens-Ole. I went for more coffee in the kitchen when he called me on my cell.

"Rebekka," I said answering it.

"Good job my girl. This is great. Good stuff. Just make sure we get that picture okay? It would really make this great. We need good pictures to sell papers. You know that."

I sipped my coffee and stared out the window. The editorial room was in the center of the town, on the main street that was closed to cars and open only for pedestrians. Tourists were walking in the street eating ice-cream cones, chatting, talking, laughing, and shopping. They

Three, Four ... Better lock your door

brought new life and lots of money to the town. Summer was the best time to be in Karrebaeksminde and this year the merchants were happy that the summer had stretched all the way into September.

"I know," I said. "Sune is on it. He'll get it. Don't worry."

"With you I never do," Jens-Ole said.

His confidence in me still surprised me. He had always had that. My guess was that that was what made him such a great leader. He trusted his employees. He made us feel proud of working for him. Come to think of it I don't think I had ever worked for a guy like him before, not even in my star-reporting days when I worked for the biggest national newspaper in Denmark. Not even back when I was a war-correspondent had I experienced such confidence in me and what I could do. It was a great feeling. It made me want to do my personal best all the time whether I was covering small town budget-negotiations or a serial killer's killing spree around this town. I wanted to do well. I wanted to make Jens-Ole happy. I had never disappointed him before.

"Have the picture in my mailbox no later than ten," he said and hung up.

I started to get nervous around nine in the evening. Sara had left at six and I ordered a pizza while I waited. I had called my dad and asked him to take care of Julie and put her to bed which he was more than happy to do, luckily for me. I hadn't heard from Sune in an hour and I really didn't want to bug him about it, but now I picked up the phone and called him again.

"Still no body?" I asked.

"Nope," he answered.

"And we're sure that it hadn't already left the inn before we arrived this morning?" I asked while knocking my pen rhythmically into the edge of the table.

"I have no idea. I've talked to the personnel and they haven't seen it leave the building, so I assume that it is still in here."

"Could they have taken it out using another exit?"

Sune sighed. "Of course they could have. Maybe the owner of the inn wanted it that way since he didn't want to lose any more guests than necessary."

I exhaled deeply. "Of course," I said.

"So what do you want me to do?" Sune asked.

"Stay a few minutes more and then leave. Who's taking care of Tobias?"

"Your dad. He called me after he talked to you. He figured that we both had to work late so he wanted to know if he should pick up both kids now he was going that way anyway. He said he had a bunch of meatballs that needed to be eaten soon, so I was really helping him out by saying yes."

I laughed. "That sounds like my dad."

"He's one of a kind."

"See you back here then. We have to send the rest of the pictures for the articles."

"Damn it!" Sune exclaimed. "I really had my heart set on that front-page."

"So had I," I said.

Half an hour later Sune still hadn't arrived. I was beginning to get worried. Could he have been in an accident on his way back? I texted him but received no answer back. I didn't want to call him since I was afraid of sounding like a worried panic-stricken mother. But at the same time I couldn't escape the thought that there was a killer on the loose somewhere in our little town.

As I stared out the window into the black darkness only lit by the streetlamps and pictured Sune being stabbed by some brown-haired tall medium-build stranger I heard footsteps on the stairs. I gasped and looked at the door. My imagination had a way of running off with me and sometimes scaring me and it did at that moment. My heart was beating fast and I grabbed a stapler from the table and was holding it tight in my hand. The steps stopped outside the door and the handle moved slowly.

I breathed heavily as the door opened. It was Sune. I exhaled relieved.

"Why are you holding a stapler?" he asked with a grin.

"Where have you been?" I asked angrily. "I thought you were dead or killed."

"Ah. I get it. You thought someone had killed me and now they were coming for you? What were you going to do? Staple the guy to death?"

"Very funny. Seriously. I thought you'd been in a car-accident or something. It takes ten minutes to get here from the inn. Why did it take you so long?"

"You asked me to stay a little longer."

"A few minutes. Not half an hour. They need the pictures from earlier today at the headquarters. Jens-Ole is pissed that we didn't get the picture of the body leaving," I said.

Sune smiled widely. "But we did."

"What? Are you telling me ...?"

"Sure," he said with a self-satisfied grin. "I wasn't about to give up just yet so after I spoke to you I ran around the main building of the inn and luckily I spotted an ambulance that had just arrived."

"That was for the body?"

## Three, Four ... Better lock your door

Sune nodded. "They must have been examining the room and the body all day for some reason since they waited to get it out until that late. But the pictures are great. Surrounded by the darkness and everything. The blue light from the ambulance is reflected in the windows of the inn. See for yourself," he said and handed me his camera.

I went through the pictures pressing the buttons on the camera frantically. He was right. They were perfect. Better than I could have hoped for. I jumped up and kissed Sune on the cheek. He blushed.

"I'm sorry," I said and pulled back realizing I had overstepped a line. "This is just really, really good. Thank you so much."

"It's my job, you know."

"I know. That's why I think you should call Jens-Ole and tell him about it. Make him happy. Let him know you were the one who saved the day. Take some credit for your work for once."

"Really? You mean it?" he asked.

"Sure."

Sune took out his phone and found the number. I heard him talk to Jens-Ole while he went out in the kitchen. I plugged the camera into my computer and started uploading the pictures. I drank my coffee very satisfied as I studied each and every one of them on my screen. When I got to the third one I put my cup down on the table. Something had caught my eye. I waited till all of the pictures were in my computer, then I opened them again and found that third one. I zoomed in to see up close what had caught my eye. Apparently the arrival of the ambulance had attracted a small crowd of what I guessed had to be neighbors or people coincidentally passing by the small street behind the inn. What caught my eye was standing right in the middle of that crowd. It was a woman. Her hair was blond and looked almost yellow in the light from the streetlamps. She was wearing a long blue gown, like an elegant evening dress for a cocktail party. It was sparkling, glittering, and reflecting the blinking light from the ambulance in front of her.

She was staring at the scene, her eyes fixated on the body bag leaving the inn on a stretcher.

It seemed that she was smiling.

## Chapter 6

My dad had prepared breakfast for us when I came down the next morning. He had done that every morning since I had moved back in with him two years ago. I smiled when I heard him hum in the kitchen as I walked down the stairs. Julie was already sitting at the table fully dressed; eating her boiled egg and buttered toast contentedly.

Dad turned and looked at me as I entered the kitchen. He was leaning on his cane, wearing Mom's old apron. The smell of bacon coming from the stove was heavenly. I couldn't help smiling. If anyone had ever told me when I was younger that my dad was going to cook for me one day I would have laughed. That had always been Mom's thing. But ever since she died and we moved in with him after my break with my ex-husband Peter he had taken it as his responsibility that we would have something good to eat.

"If I left it up to your mother you would be eating all that Asian food or pizza all the time," he said once to Julie.

I guess he was right, I thought as I sat down on a chair next to Julie. I wasn't much of a cook and to be honest I really didn't want to be one of those moms who baked cookies and cooked homemade meals every day. I mean I had the deepest respect for those who could do such a thing, but I think I just never had the patience for it. Everything always went wrong when I tried and I really, really hated it. Some people just weren't cut out to be great cooks, I kept telling myself.

"Eggs?" Dad asked.

"Sure," I said and handed him my plate. Several times I had asked if he wanted me to cook every now and then so he didn't have to do it all the time, but he had politely refused by telling me that I would only "mess the place up." Little by little I had realized that he wasn't just being stubborn about it, cooking for us was actually good for him. Taking care of his family got him out of bed in the morning. It gave him a purpose. He seemed to be enjoying that a lot. I had even at one point suggested that Julie and I should get our own apartment so we wouldn't be a burden to him any longer, but I quickly regretted doing so. The expression on my dad's face said it all. The prospect of losing us, of us moving away from him, out of this house - was of catastrophic dimensions. He never said it in words, but I knew it once I saw that look in his eyes. If we moved out he would grow old in a heartbeat. He needed us as much as we needed him.

"There is coffee in the pot," he said and pointed at the machine in the corner.

"Thanks dad." I got up and poured myself a cup, sat back down and looked at Julie. She was reading a magazine about horses. I sipped my coffee and tasted the scrambled eggs he always made especially for me. Lots of butter in them, and whole milk the way Dad always made them. It was delicious.

"So horses, huh?" I asked Julie and looked at the magazine.

Julie smiled. "Yes. I really, really loves horses, mommy. I want to learn how to ride horses. Can I Mom?"

I exhaled and leaned back. "But I just paid for a whole year of gymnastics, and you love gymnastics. I don't know anything about horses. All I know is that it is extremely expensive, and I really don't think I can afford it."

"Come on, Mom. Please? I really want to ride horses."

I put my hand on top of hers. "And you really, really wanted to do gymnastics a couple of months ago and you would do anything if I would let you go, remember? I've paid for an entire year so you're sticking with it. Then maybe next year if you still want to learn how to ride horses I'll consider it."

"That's not fair," Julie said and threw her fork on the plate.

"Well it's fair to me," I argued.

But Julie was beyond reasoning and solid arguments. She had set her heart on this thing.

"Why do you hate me so much?" she asked.

She was pulling the pity-card. It was my own fault that she had become so spoiled. When I was still married to her father he had spoiled her a lot and I had always been the bad guy, but once we split up and I had to move her far away I felt so bad for her that I gave her anything she set her heart on. Especially after her dad decided he couldn't see her any longer. I felt sick to my stomach because I knew she was hurting inside, missing him badly and not understanding why he didn't want to see her. But he was sick. "Daddy is really sick and needs to go away to get well," I told her.

"Well, I don't hate you," I said to Julie. "I love you very much, but you can't make me pay for an entire year of gymnastics and then bail on it a month later. I'll lose all the money I have already paid."

"It's always about the money with you," she mumbled.

"Well money is important. I don't want you thinking that you can just throw money around as you please. I work hard to earn it."

"Tobias is doing it," she said. "His dad said he can start next week."

"Tobias is learning how to ride horses?" I asked surprised. Now I understood how the idea had suddenly appeared in her head and why I hadn't heard anything about this before.

"I bet Tobias' dad hasn't just paid for a whole year of gymnastics as well."

Now Julie was crying. "I can never do anything; you never let me do anything that I want to do. I already told you that I don't want to do gymnastics anymore," she exclaimed loudly.

I opened my mouth to talk when I was suddenly interrupted by Dad. "You know what sweetie-pie?" he asked.

"No," she sniffed.

"I'll pay for those riding-lessons. I can take you there and bring you back. Now wasn't that a good solution?"

I almost choked in my coffee while Julie started smiling widely. "No, Dad. You can't do that. I just said no," I argued not believing how he could be so insensitive to me.

Julie's smile froze. She stared at me with contempt. "You can't do that! If grand-dad wants to give me the riding lessons then you can't just take them back."

"I can and I will," I said.

Julie stood up and pushed her chair backwards. "I hate you!" she yelled and ran up the stairs.

I exhaled and looked at Dad. He shook his head.

"What?" I said. "I have to stand my ground with her. She is getting way too spoiled around here. You can't undermine my authority like that when I have just said no to her. It's not fair to me, Dad. I'm trying to discipline her and teach her the value of money. If she starts riding lessons this month, she will want something else next month."

"I know what you're trying to do," he said. "But for God's sake, she misses her dad like crazy, school is tough on her, the girls are picking on her both in school and at gymnastics, she doesn't have much that makes her happy except Tobias. She wants to start riding lessons to be with him more. So she'll know she at least has one friend."

I swallowed hard trying to oppress the feeling of guilt growing inside of me. "How come I didn't know this? Why isn't she telling me that herself?"

"Because she is afraid you'll think there is something wrong with her. She wants to be perfect for you. She wants to be like you. Strong and independent. She wants you to be proud of her and she thinks you won't be if she is not doing well in school and doing well at her age means being popular and having lots of friends."

"So she's embarrassed because the other girls are nasty to her?" I asked.

Dad nodded. "I think so."

I smiled and stared at my father standing in front of me in Mom's old apron and with a spatula in his hand.

"How did you become so smart?" I asked.

"I had two daughters of my own, remember?"

"Vaguely."

I drove a very mute Julie to school and then headed to the office where Sune was waiting for me. I waved at Sara and walked towards him.

"We have ten minutes to get to the press conference," he said, looking at his watch. "We can make it if we leave right away."

"Really? Horses?" I asked. "Couldn't you have found something say a little less expensive?"

"I'm sorry," Sune said shrugging. "It was Tobias' idea and I thought it would be great for him to do a sport that involved animals and fresh air."

"I guess it is kind of healthy for them. It's just so annoying. I just paid for an entire year of gymnastics for Julie and now she wants to do this instead."

"Contact them and tell them that Julie changed her mind and say you want a refund," he said. "It's worth a try."

I exhaled. "I guess you're right. I just really hate to give in to her once I have said no to something."

Sune picked up his bag with his camera and many lenses. We started walking. He held the door for me. "I know," he said. "You're too proud."

## Chapter 7

THE PRESS CONFERENCE WAS HELD IN A BIG CONFERENCE ROOM AT the police station. To my surprise the room was packed. TV cameras were in place, journalists with microphones and notepads were swarming around. I was quite startled that a killing in our little part of the country could attract that kind of attention. But it also meant that my editor would be thrilled because we were first with the story.

With my own paper in my hand I sat in the middle of the crowd and prepared my questions by writing them on my notepad. Sune walked around and took pictures of the scenery of people getting ready and waiting.

"Is this seat taken?" a male voice asked me.

I lifted my head and looked into a pair of very blue eyes.

I shook my head. "I don't think so," I said.

"Then you won't mind me taking it?"

I smiled politely. "Go ahead."

The man sat down next to me while I continued my preparations.

"Hi, I am Christian, by the way," he said and held out his hand. "Christian Lonstedt."

I took it. "Rebekka," I said.

"Ah. Rebekka Franck?" he said and took out a paper. He showed me the front page and my article and Sune's picture of the body bag leaving the scene. He pointed at my picture next to my name. "Yes. I recognize you now. You were first with the story huh?"

I smiled again politely. The guy looked at me with a wide smile showing pearly white teeth. He was annoyingly good-looking. "Very nice to meet you," he said.

"I haven't seen you before, who do you work for?" I asked.

"I'm with the *Express*. I work at the department in Naestved. I cover all of South Zealand."

"What happened to Frederik Hansen?"

"He's still there. They just expanded the staff," Christian answered.

I nodded as the door opened and the officer from the day before entered followed by four men in uniform. They all sat at the long table equipped with microphones. The officer I had spoken to at the inn was the new head of police in Karrebaeksminde, on the sign in front of him his name Johannes Lindstroem was written in golden letters. He started talking.

"Yesterday this town was a witness to a horrible crime. A woman, Susanne Larsen from Naestved was found killed in her hotel room at Astrupgaard Inn by the cleaning personnel at nine forty-five Thursday morning. The room was booked in her name. She was last seen eating dinner with a man in the restaurant, you should all have a description of the man we're seeking lying on your seat."

There was a murmur while people picked up the piece of paper provided by the police.

"It is not much, as you can tell, but it is the only lead we have so far. There are no surveillance cameras that caught these two together nor are there any records of who he is anywhere. He could be anybody. Still we would appreciate it if you could all mention his description and tell people to contact us if they think they know this guy."

Johannes Lindstroem paused and looked at the crowd. "This case is a precarious matter to us, since the deceased was married to one of our fellow officers from Naestved. They had two children. I am personally determined to hunt this killer down if it is the last thing I'll ever do." He paused again. "Therefore we have decided to work together with Naestved police on this case. It has the highest priority now. Any questions?"

A forest of hands reached towards the ceiling. "Yes, Rebekka Franck. Let's begin with you since you were the first with the story."

"Do you have a murder-weapon?" I said. "Do you know how she was killed?"

"We are still waiting for the forensic-report."

"So you didn't find a weapon in her room or know what kind you are looking for?" I asked again.

"Not yet, no. I don't want to go into details about the modus operandi until we have the report that determines exactly how she died."

"Do the police know what Susanne Larsen was doing at the inn?"

Johannes Lindstroem shook his head. "I am not sure why that's important?"

"If she lives in Naestved only fifteen minutes away from here, why was she spending the night at Astrupgaard?"

Johannes Lindstroem sighed. "I think that goes under privacy of the family."

"But is it something you're investigating? She met with a man and had dinner, could it have been a jealous scorned boyfriend or lover?"

Johannes Lindstroem exhaled. "I think we should move on," he said and pointed at another journalist.

I leaned back in the chair while noting on my pad. I couldn't help escaping the thought that if Susanne Larsen had been at the inn with her secret lover then the most obvious killer would be her own husband, the police officer from Naestved and close friend of Johannes Lindstroem.

I wrote the article about the press-conference as soon as we got back to the office. Sune uploaded the pictures and we picked out a few to send to my editor along with the story. The focus was the woman being the wife of a police officer and how the head of the police in Karrebaeksminde now regarded this case as highest priority and that he was determined to "hunt this killer down even if it was the last thing he ever did" and that he intended to do so with help from Naestved police department. The story came out pretty good and had that human touch to it, that this now was a personal matter for the police.

I pressed the 'send' button and went for coffee in the kitchen. I came back with a piece of marble-cake for both Sune and me. Sara already had her share, I could tell by the empty plate next to her with cake crumbs on it.

Minutes later Jens-Ole was on the phone. "Great piece on the conference. I want you to find the husband," he said. "I want an interview with him about how horrible this last twenty-four hours has been."

I dropped my head. I hated those kinds of interviews. Seeking the poor fellow left behind in his grief and asking him how he felt. It was so low. It was something the Express would do. They would stoop that low because they had no morals or integrity.

"Really?" I asked. "Isn't that a little low for us?"

"Don't start getting ethical on me. If you're too proud to do real journalism and dig in where it hurts, then I'm sure I can find someone else to do it. Do you agree? I'm sure you do. I want the story in the paper tomorrow."

Then he hung up. I sighed.

"Now what?" asked Sune.

"Jens-Ole wants us to find the husband," I answered.

Sune shrugged. "Then let's do it," he said cheerfully. "Have Sara find him while we drive there."

"I'm already on it," Sara said from behind her desk.

Then Sune put his arm around my shoulder and started humming while we walked. I smiled after a few reluctant steps. Then I hummed along with him.

"See it doesn't hurt that bad to swallow some of that pride every now and then," he said with a grin while he held the door to the car for me.

"I'm driving," I said and grabbed the car keys from his hand with a grin.

Sune shrugged and jumped in the passenger seat. We drove off to the humming sound of "Fly me to the moon" coming from Sune's mouth.

## Chapter 8

It was late before we got home. Sune and I had spent all day in Naestved talking to Bjarne Larsen, Susanne Larsen's husband who naturally was devastated over losing his wife. He had agreed to give me the interview after fifteen minutes of persuasion from me. Eventually I convinced him that it would make the police's work easier if the public had a face to relate to, someone they felt like they were helping.

Bjarne Larsen had been reluctant but friendly and little by little he opened up and talked about how horrible it had been to have the officers coming to his door and telling him what had happened, that now he knew what it was like to be on the other side, to be the one being told that something bad had happened to your loved one.

I listened carefully to his every word and while Sune took pictures of the husband but not the children as I had instructed him to. I wrote every word Bjarne Larsen said on my note-pad. He told me how wonderful a wife and mother Susanne was, how much she would be missed by him and the kids and what a great nurse she was at the hospital where she had worked for almost twenty years. How devoted she was to her patients. She had known already when she was very young that she wanted to be a nurse and help people. It was like a calling for her.

I nodded along and wrote it all down. It was good stuff and would make an excellent article. By the end of the interview I finally found the courage to ask the one question that had been on my mind for quite a while now.

"What was your wife doing at the inn in Karrebaeksminde?"

Bjarne Larsen's moustache vibrated on his lip.

"Excuse me?" he asked.

"Was she visiting someone? Why was she at the inn?" I asked again as politely as I could manage.

Bjarne Larsen paused for long time. He dropped his eyes.

"Where did she tell you she was going?" I asked.

The small man in front of me shrank in the couch. "To see her sister in Nakskov," he mumbled.

I nodded. "Sounds like a private matter," I said. "I won't put that in the paper. Don't worry."

Bjarne Larsen nodded slowly. "Thanks."

As promised I didn't put anything about it in the article I wrote once Sune and I got back to the office. There was no need to kick a man already lying down. The article was strong enough as it was and less than an hour later I sent it to Jens-Ole and as soon as he had approved it, Sune and I drove back home to where both of our kids were sleeping upstairs in Julie's room. The floor was packed with Barbie-horses and horse magazines and cartoons about girls horse-back-riding.

"Busy day, huh?" I said to Sune as we watched them both sleeping in Julie's bed.

"I bet it has been," Sune replied.

"Let him stay here," I said when Sune was about to go pick up Tobias from the bed. "It's a weekend. There's no school tomorrow. They'll play all day."

Sune smiled. "Thanks," he said. "Tobias really enjoys coming here. He doesn't have many friends."

"Neither does Julie. Do you want a glass of red wine?" I asked as we walked down the stairs. Dad had fallen asleep on the couch in front of the television. I turned it off and put a blanket over him. "It's a nice night. We could sit outside on the porch."

"Sure," Sune said. "With a jacket and some blankets wrapped around us we could probably stay warm enough."

"Great." I went into the kitchen and grabbed a bottle and two wine glasses while Sune found blankets around in the house and carried them outside.

One bottle soon became two and not long after I was getting tipsy. It was nice sitting outside with Sune and talking. He always made me feel so comfortable. With him I could always be myself completely.

"Whatever happened to that Italian guy that you used to date? The one who was an artist?" Sune asked.

I scoffed. "Let's just say it's over."

"I kind of figured that one out, but what happened?"

"He was an ass. He was nice in the beginning but he was the type that liked the hunt. As soon as he felt sure of me he started acting like an idiot. I made the mistake to have him meet Julie and she wasn't happy about me meeting a new guy so soon after her dad. Plus Giovanni didn't like kids. He didn't want to have her as a part of his life. So naturally I had to end it."

"I bet he didn't like that much," Sune laughed.

"Nope. Wasn't good for his ego. Apparently he had never had a woman say no to him before. He claimed he had never been dumped."

"What an idiot," Sune exclaimed and sipped his wine.

"My words exactly," I said and paused. "What about you?"

"What about me?"

"I have known you for two years now and I have never heard about any women in your life."

"I have you," he said laughing. "You're the only woman in my life. You and Julie of course."

I drank some more wine and stared at the starry night in front of us. It had gotten really cold now but it was such a beautiful clear night and I didn't want it to end. I inhaled the crispy air.

"Here," Sune said and wrapped his arm and his blanket around me. I was leaning my head on him. He smelled good. I had never thought about it but he was actually quite good-looking underneath all the black make-up and the Mohawk. He had a pretty face and spectacular eyes. "You'll find someone," I said.

Then he looked at me and I suddenly had the oddest feeling inside of me. My fear was confirmed when he leaned over and grabbed my chin. He lifted my face till my lips met his. Then we kissed. Tenderly, awaiting at first, then aggressively and demanding.

I pulled away. "Sune. We can't do this," I said. My head was spinning from the wine. I had drunk too much, I let my guard down. I sat up and pulled away from him. "This was really stup ..." Sune grabbed my neck and pulled my face close to his again. Then he kissed me passionately. Like he had wanted to do this for years, yearned, longed for this to happen. I kissed him back for a few seconds before I managed to push him away.

"Sune. We really can't do this," I repeated.

"Why not?" he muttered under his breath. "Why?"

"Because we work together. Because we have children. Because you're ten years younger than me. You should find some nice girl your own age. Not an old hag like me."

Sune got up from the couch we had been sitting on. There was hurt in his eyes when he looked at me. "So I'm too young?"

"No. Yes. Well it's not just ... for Christ sake, Sune. We work together."

"I'd better go now," he said.

"Don't leave mad," I said.

He bit his lip. "No, no it's okay. I understand. You don't want me." He paused. "I'll come and get Tobias tomorrow."

"Sune. Don't leave. Let's talk about this ..."

But Sune had already turned his back to me and left.

## Chapter 9

ANDERS HOEJMARK HAD LOVED BADMINTON ALL HIS LIFE. IT WASN'T so much the game itself as it was the social aspect of it. It was a great way to meet people. At the local club in Karrebaeksminde Anders Hoejmark met many in his job as president. Club members called him 'Mr. President' when they met him inside of the hall, or in the cafeteria. They would greet him with a smile and say "Hello Mr. President. The kids would yell it as well. "Hi Mr. President" and he would pat them on their heads and ask them if they were going to grow up to be as big as the Danish players Camilla Martin or Peter Gade who had been among the world's best players.

He enjoyed it immensely. The respect, the authority he had in this club. Being the daily leader gave him so much more joy than any other job he had before. Whenever he stepped inside this sports center he was in charge. He was the king. He would tell the cleaning crew that they had done a great job in the dressing rooms or that they needed to take care of the men's restrooms one more time since someone just messed it up, because people were sometimes so gross - even the nice people attending this sports center. Some of the younger punks would throw paper towels in the toilet and clog it. He would track them down and punish them that was certain. He would ban them from the center for a month if they didn't behave or follow the rules. He threatened to call their parents if necessary. If they pleaded and begged him not to tell? Then he would let them pay right there on the spot. He would drag them to his office and lower the shades. Then he would unzip his pants and have them give him a blow-job.

After that they would be off the hook. Until next time they did something to piss him off. There was always someone who would get in trouble. Anders Hoejmark saw it as his duty to teach them a lesson.

Yes, badminton was a wonderful way to meet new people, Anders Hoejmark thought to himself as he walked through the cafeteria greeting people with smiles and nods. They were serving meatballs with mashed potato today and he wouldn't miss it for the world. Friday night was always a busy night at the sports center and it never closed until nine. He took in a deep breath and filled his nostrils with the scent of sweat as he walked by a group of young boys sitting around a table with their rackets in bags standing next to them. One of them dropped a pack of feather balls in front of Anders so they were scattered all over the floor. Anders Hoejmark stopped and sighed deeply. The young man gasped. Anders Hoejmark smiled. Then he patted the boy's head.

"Just make sure you pick them all up," he said and moved along towards the line. Normally he would have said something worse to the young man, but not today. Today was a good day and a busy one as well.

As he glanced through the room his eyes met with those of a man. Anders Hoejmark felt excited on the inside. Those eyes did that to him. He had only known him a week, since the man had started coming in the club and they had only spoken a few times, but Anders Hoejmark had no doubts. This man was someone special. He was different than anyone he had ever met before. This could very well evolve into something bigger. Normally when Anders Hoejmark met guys like him at the club they would meet once or twice in the men's dressing room and have casual sex and then they would never speak again. That was usually how it went. But this time Anders Hoejmark had a feeling that this could be more than just a fling, more than a one-night stand. Even if he hadn't known the man for long and never spoken more than a few sentences with him he knew that he could love this man. He could fall for him. Right now they shared a secret so delightful Anders Hoejmark had a difficult time containing it. They were going to finally meet. Later this day, tonight.

Anders Hoejmark had spotted him one day a week ago when he had been playing with another man in the hall. He had seen him from his office upstairs that had a view over the entire arena and all the nets. He had seen the man and studied his physique; every fiber and muscle in his body and Anders Hoejmark had a hard time restraining himself. He was so incredibly attracted to the man physically at that moment. He wanted him, he wanted to touch those muscular arms and massage those beautiful legs. He wanted to nibble his ears and kiss his neck.

But the man was way out of his league, and straight too, he had thought sadly to himself. There was no way he would be interested in a bald old man like Anders Hoejmark. He had stared at himself in the mirror at the restroom and sighed.

Love hadn't been easy for Anders Hoejmark. It had in fact been almost non-existent in his life. If it was because he was gay or because he had no idea how to love others, he didn't know. But one thing he did know: he didn't love himself. He hadn't been able to stand himself ever since ... since. He knew there was no use in hanging on to the past. It was twenty years ago and he had gotten away with it.

"Still you have to live with it the rest of his life," he told his reflection in the men's restroom mirror. He would have cried in self-pity if the door hadn't opened at that very moment and the man had stepped in. Anders Hoejmark gasped at the sight of his face behind him in the mirror. The man smiled the most charming smile, and then he came really close to Anders Hoejmark. He had gently touched his neck and caressed his face and hair. A shiver of almost orgasmic proportions had gone through Anders Hoejmark's body. Then the man had leaned over him and whispered in his ear.

"I want to meet with you."

Anders Hoejmark had gasped at the sound of his voice so close to his ear. Everything about this man was so desirable.

"The men's dressing room next Friday after I've closed the center. I'll leave the back-door open," Anders Hoejmark whispered with quivering voice.

The man smiled in the mirror and then licked the back of Anders Hoejmark's ear causing him to tremble with desire and lust for him right then and there. Anders Hoejmark had closed his eyes taking in every second of this moment.

When he opened them the man was gone.

## Chapter 10

Friday had finally arrived. Anders Hoejmark was whistling as he finished his meatballs and mashed potato in his office while watching the players sweat and throw themselves around on the court to strike the feathered shuttlecock or birdie as some preferred to call it. It was indeed a beautiful game. And the Danish league was known to be one of the strongest in the world. Anders Hoejmark was proud to be a part of something this big something the entire nation could be proud of. He loved everything about it: the aerodynamics of the shuttlecock, the athletic players, the sweat on the player's foreheads, the tight shorts. He used to play it himself. When he was a child it had always been the source of much joy. Even if he didn't play any longer it still provided joy into his life, he thought and looked at his watch. It was almost nine and about time to close up, he thought with a thrill. He watched as the players finished their last game and started to pack up. They disappeared into the dressing rooms for a little while then returned with wet hair and clean clothes. They were laughing, chatting as they left the sports center one by one and soon Anders Hoejmark felt the silence slowly fall upon the great gymnasium. He loved these moments just as much as he enjoyed it when the center was filled with people. The quiet moments and the anticipation were both precious as well.

Anders Hoejmark went on his usual rounds. First he checked the cafeteria to see if the lady had remembered to shut off everything. He had heard of a gymnasium in Holte that burned down because someone forgot to shut off the fryer. Ever since then he had made it a habit to check all the equipment in the kitchen to make sure nothing could burn it all down. He checked the coffeemaker, the fryer, the pan, the toaster, everything. Anders Hoejmark was a very thorough man so even if he was in a hurry this day to get to the dressing room and get ready for his date he didn't slack on the security. After the cafeteria he locked all the doors - except the backdoor of course. He put in a small piece of wood to keep it open so the man would know that this was the door. With a thrill of excitement running through his body Anders Hoejmark checked the last things, made sure that all shuttlecocks were picked up, and forgotten towels, shirts and shorts put in the lost-and-found box by the entrance for people to find next time they arrived to play.

Then he could finally enter the men's dressing room. He put some water on his hands and washed his face. Then he combed the last remains of hair he had, trying to cover as much as possible of his growing baldness. He was sweating and wiped his face with paper towels. It wasn't like him to be this nervous. This meeting had to be something special. It felt like such a defining moment in his life. Like this was the moment that could change his life forever. Finally he had met someone he could imagine having a real relationship with.

Anders Hoejmark glanced around the room and suddenly regretted the surroundings he had chosen for their first meeting. He should have chosen something better, something signaling that he wanted more than casual sex. But Anders Hoejmark wanted both. He wanted the rough casual sex as well as the romance and love. Up until now he had only known the first; he had never experienced the second part. He had no idea how to go about it, how to do that. But maybe the man would know? Maybe he could show him how to love? Anders Hoejmark hoped it and wished for this to happen so deeply that every fiber in his body craved it. This was it.

It was now or never.

When the door opened to the dressing room Anders Hoejmark smiled and turned around feeling his heart racing in his chest and the adrenalin rushing through his veins.

Then he froze. The sight of a tall woman in a blue evening-gown made his body feel heavy like stone.

I should have known, he thought to himself. I should have known that I wasn't going to get away with this after all. I should have known that the past would come back to haunt me some day.

It always does.

She was moving slowly towards him raising the scalpel in her hand. She reached out with the other hand and grabbed Anders Hoejmark by the throat. He tried to fight her, but she was too strong. Almost supernaturally strong.

"Please," he pleaded half choked. "It's been twenty years."

The woman didn't speak, she only giggled like a little girl as she cornered Anders Hoejmark against the light blue tiles in the bath where he had so often enjoyed the secret pleasures of the flesh with fleeting acquaintances. His deadly screams were echoed in the gymnasium as the scalpel went slowly through the skin of his forehead.

## Chapter 11

BRIAN POULSEN WAS TIRED. HE ALWAYS WAS THESE DAYS. HECK HE had always been. Twenty-three and he could never get out of bed in time. Not back when he was in school, before they threw him out, not when he had his first job at an auto repair shop that his mom had gotten for him and that he later was fired from. No Brian Poulsen had never been an early riser and he certainly wasn't this Saturday morning when he had to get out of bed and go to the sports center across town to open the doors for the group of telemarketing workers that had rented the gymnasium for two hours as part of the company's yearly picnic and "get-together" for all its workers.

Brian Poulsen did not enjoy having to leave his warm bed on a Saturday morning at eight thirty after a night playing Diablo III on his computer. But he had to. There was no way he could screw this one up his social worker had told him. If he wanted to continue receiving his social welfare he had to take this job. It was part of his "activation-package" that the county had ordered for all people on welfare. Brian Poulsen found it ridiculous. All these rules and regulations didn't help him one bit. It only made him resent working even more. Now he had to get up every weekend and open the gymnasium for people who seriously wanted to spend their Saturdays and Sundays chasing a stupid feather-shuttlecock around a small court. Just because the leader of the place wanted to be able to sleep in during the weekends. Brian Poulsen cursed the leader as he parked the bike in the rack in front of the sports center. He sighed and shivered. It was cold this morning even if it had been warm the day before. It was definitely going to be fall soon. Brian Poulsen couldn't wait for the cold to come back. He didn't care much for summer. He hated spending time outdoors. Why people insisted on going to the

## Three, Four ... Better lock your door

beach and running around half-naked in the parks, he never understood. He didn't even like barbeque so he always refused if his parents invited him while he was at their house to give his mom the weekly bag of laundry. Brian Poulsen would rather just order in a pizza and play on his computer.

"Is that all you're ever going to do with your life?" his mother would ask with worry in her eyes.

He would answer by shrugging. He really didn't know. He had no ambitions or any dreams for his life. He used to though. He had dreamed about becoming a writer. But then he had written a short-story in high school and his teacher had absolutely hated it. Told him he would do the world a huge favor by never writing anything again. It just wasn't for him. It wasn't his thing.

Brian Poulsen found the key to the entrance of the gymnasium and opened it with a deep sigh. It wasn't that bad a job after all, he thought to himself. He walked from door to door and unlocked each and every one. When he came to the door in the back of the building he was surprised that it was already open. Not just unlocked like someone had forgotten to lock it, but propped open with a small piece of wood. On the broad handle Brian Poulsen discovered something else. Something was on it. He touched it and felt disgusted.

It was blood.

Thinking that someone probably just hurt themselves while playing badminton he wiped the blood off his hand in his pants with repulsion then continued opening up the gymnasium and went into the cafeteria where he turned on all the machines: the coffeemaker, the fryer, the pan, the toaster. Simply making sure that everything was ready for the lady who worked there when she arrived at nine. Then he walked downstairs onto the courts and swept them with a mop to make sure there was no old sweat or dirt on them. He unlocked the cabinets with extra shuttlecocks and racquets. He found clean towels and took out a new pack of paper towels and went towards the dressing room. He had his hands full so he had to push the door open with his back. Brian Poulsen yawned a few times as he walked inside and put the towels on a bench. Then he opened the pack of paper towels and took them out ready to fill up the container next to the sink.

When he lifted his head and looked into the mirror he saw more blood smeared all over the light blue tiles in the bath. Brian Poulsen turned his head slowly; his heart was beating fast in his chest. What he saw next made him gasp for breath and drop the paper towels, scattering them all over the floor.

## Chapter 12

I woke up with a headache. It had to be all that wine; I thought and went into the bathroom to take a quick shower. The water felt nice on my body and slowly I woke up.

Julie and Tobias were still sleeping in her room when I checked on them afterwards. I sighed and got dressed while remembering the night before with Sune on the porch. I really hoped that this wasn't going to be a problem between the two of us. I loved working with him and enjoyed his company immensely. I really didn't want to lose him. I was afraid that this thing would come between us.

I brushed my hair and looked at my face in the mirror. I was getting older. The last couple of years had been hard on me. That Sune in any way had interest in me romantically was a huge surprise to me. I was an old woman compared to him. He was in his twenties and should find a girl the same age and with the same interests as him. We were nothing alike if you thought about it. All we had in common was our job. He couldn't possibly be interested in me could he? He had in no way shown that before. It was actually quite a shock. What was more shocking to me was that I enjoyed his kiss. I liked it.

I exhaled and put the brush down. But it could never be. I might have liked the kiss but I wasn't interested in him like that. How could I be?

I heard Julie and Tobias wake up in their room next to mine and stuck my head through the door.

"Morning guys. Slept well?"

They both smiled and nodded drowsily.

"I am going downstairs to eat now. See you in the kitchen?"

"Sure," Tobias answered.

## Three, Four ... Better lock your door

I closed the door feeling nervous inside. Would this cause a problem in our children's relationship? What if Sune didn't want to see us anymore and therefore didn't want to let Tobias come here anymore? My heart was heavy as I walked downstairs. Dad was whistling in the kitchen. It was the best sound in the world, I thought to myself. He was so happy with our arrangement. What was I ever going to do once he wasn't here anymore? I pushed the thought out of my head. I didn't want to think about that now.

"Morning sweetheart," Dad said and kissed me on the cheek.

"Morning," I answered and poured myself a cup of coffee.

I sat at the table and took a sip of coffee. Dad had been to the bakery and brought back freshly baked bread rolls and pastries. He placed a bowl of soft-boiled eggs in front of me. I took a roll and buttered it.

A few minutes later Julie and Tobias came down the stairs. Their hair looked messy from sleeping. They were both smiling. They were always so happy when they were together. I enjoyed having Tobias at the house. He had become the brother I had never given Julie. I had always wanted more than one child. I wanted an entire bunch of them. But now I didn't know any longer. I certainly didn't want any more children with Peter, Julie's dad. He was way too unstable. But would I want them with someone else? I couldn't imagine who that should be. I couldn't imagine myself being pregnant and going through all that stuff once again.

Dad served them rolls and juice. I was going through the newspapers as I always did in the morning. Making sure no other paper had a story that we should have done before them.

"When am I going home today?" Tobias asked.

I put down the paper and looked at him. "I don't know, sweetie. I told your dad to let you stay for a few hours, giving you some time to play."

Tobias and Julie cheered and looked at each other with great excitement.

"That means we can go in our secret hide-out and finish the game," Julie whispered so loudly everyone around the table could hear it.

"What secret hide-out?" I asked.

"If I told you it wouldn't be a secret," Julie said with a smile. Then she whispered to Tobias, "Hurry up and finish your breakfast so we can play."

Tobias shoveled in his rolls and washed it all down with his orange juice, causing him to cough.

"Easy there," I said. "Can't have you choking."

Tobias threw me a smile to ensure me he was fine. Then they ran off.

"What about your plates?" I yelled after them. "You know you have to clean up after yourselves."

But they were long gone. I took their plates and put them in the dishwasher.

"What's that about a secret hide-out?" I asked Dad.

He shrugged with a mischievous smile. Then he shook his head. "If I told you it wouldn't be a secret," he said.

"Are you on their side now?" I asked.

"I think I have always been on their side."

"Hmm," I said. "As long as you know that they're not getting themselves into any kind of trouble in there," I said and went back to my paper.

"What kind of trouble?"

I lifted my head from the paper and looked into the eyes of Sune. He turned his head as our eyes met.

"Sune!" Dad exclaimed. "Come on in. Have a bite to eat."

Sune shook his head. "I really can't. I'm just here to pick up Tobias."

I exhaled. "So soon? I thought we agreed they could have the day to play together. It's Saturday."

"I know what day it is. I just really need to bring him home now." His voice was cold and dismissive.

"Do you have anywhere to be? Is there something you need to do today?" I asked. "I don't understand why ... You didn't say anything about this yesterday."

"You know what? It is really none of your business," Sune said.

"How about a cup of coffee?" Dad asked.

Sune shook his head again. His eyes were still avoiding mine. "No thanks. I'm good." He went towards the stairs. "Are they up there?"

Dad nodded. Sune started walking. I got up and followed him. As he reached the end of the stairs I grabbed his arm.

"Sune. Please don't do this. Don't punish the kids for what happened yesterday. It was a simple mistake. I'm willing to forget. I have already forgotten all about it. It's no big deal. It really isn't."

He turned and looked at me. His eyes were cold and distant. It scared me. His eyes were normally so warm and caring. "It might not have been a big deal for you and you might be able to forget it easily. But I can't. Not like that. I don't run around kissing girls every day. I never expose myself like I did last night. You hurt me. I will get over it eventually, but it will not be easy."

I stepped backwards and let go of his arm. "But ... but. What about work? We have to work together."

"I need this job and you need a great photographer who understands how you think. We need each other, so we will have to make this work. I see no other way. But for now I'll ask you to forgive me, but I need some space. I need to keep you at a distance."

It was like someone had ripped a part of me out when he spoke those words. I knew I was going to miss his friendship terribly, but I also knew that he was right. Keeping a distance and staying strictly professional for a while was the only way we could save this.

I just didn't know if it was possible.

"Why are you here so soon?" Tobias said.

They had heard us and started walking down the stairs.

"I've come to take you home now, Tobias. We need to go," Sune said.

Julie's expression changed drastically. I walked up to her and hugged her. "But Mom, we were supposed to ..."

"I know sweetie, but Tobias has to go home with his dad now, so you'll have to play another time."

"Dad?" Tobias said with a reproaching tone. "Can't we at least stay for a few minutes more so Julie and I can finish playing?"

I felt angry at Sune. This was ridiculous. The kids hadn't done anything wrong. There was no reason for them to be punished because their parents had acted foolishly.

Sune exhaled. I saw the hurt in his eyes. He didn't want to split the kids apart either. But somehow he felt he had to. He had to separate our lives. I understood that. I didn't applaud it but I respected his wish.

"You'll see each other in school on Monday," I said.

Julie hugged my hand tight as we waved goodbye to Sune and Tobias. It was like she somehow knew that something was going on.

"Let's play Scrabble," I said forcing a cheerful voice.

"I'd rather play Monopoly," she said.

I didn't pay much attention to the game while we were playing. I was thinking constantly about Sune and how to make this up to him. If only there was some way I could make him feel better, make him forget that stupid kiss, that entire stupid evening. I cursed myself for asking if he wanted a glass of wine. If I had only let him go home like he wanted to. If I had not let him kiss me.

Julie noticed quickly that I wasn't all there.

"Mom," she said sneering. "You're not even listening."

"Sorry. What, honey?"

"You're going to jail."

"Oh? I am? Well that's a shame."

Julie tilted her head and sighed annoyed. "Mom. You're losing the game. If you don't pay more attention I'll win."

I nodded with a smile. "That's nice honey."

Julie sighed again. My phone was in the charger at the kitchen table when it started ringing. "Just a second," I said and got up from the table. "I'd better get that."

It was Sara. That could only mean one thing. I had to work.

"Yes?"

"There's been another one," she said.

"Another one what?"

"Another killing. They found a body at the local badminton club."

"How do you know it was a killing?" I asked.

"It's a code Seventy-two, they say."

"And that means exactly what?" I looked at Julie who was moving all the pieces around on the board continuing the game without me.

"Over the years I have gotten to know all the codes. They use letters and numbers so people listening in like myself won't understand it. Like fifty-three is a DUI, twenty-three is hazardous driving; AIT is 'an accident in traffic,' CFC is 'cake for the coffee.' That means they want a patrol to bring back a cake from the bakery. A seventy-two is a homicide. Last time I heard them use that term was when Susanne Larsen was found at the inn. I've already called Sune. He'll meet you outside the club."

## Chapter 13

THE SPORTS-CENTER WAS BLOCKED BY POLICE CARS AND CRIME TAPE, when I arrived. The blue van belonging to the forensic team was parked right outside of the entrance door. I got out of the car and spotted Sune who was already taking pictures of the police at work by the back door, dressed in their suits and gloves. They were searching the area around the backdoor, slowly, methodically without talking, picking up small things with tweezers and putting them in small plastic bags for the forensic team to look at in the lab later. Some were dusting for fingerprints on the door and marking spots where blood was smeared on the handle. I pointed at the handle and asked Sune to take pictures of it.

"Already got it," he whispered.

I nodded while noting on my pad all the details of what I saw. I wanted this to be a kind of "on the scene reportage" so details were of the essence. Someone found a shoeprint. I tugged Sune's shoulder and pointed. He took pictures while they did an imprint. Sune made sure to stay on the right side of the crime tape to not bother them while they were working. I smiled. He was a true professional; it would be hard for me without him. He was so right. We needed each other. We needed to make this work.

In the door I spotted Officer Johannes Lindstroem. I waved at him eagerly and soon he saw me. He finished his conversation off and walked towards me.

"Listen," he started. "I don't know how you and your colleagues get your information this fast, but I have no comments so far. You'll have to wait till we are done here and actually have something meaningful to report to you."

"Who was killed?" I asked ignoring his remarks.

"You'll have to wait," he said. "I don't have time right now."

"Does this killing have any relation to the death of Susanne Larsen?" I asked.

He started walking.

I yelled after him. "Hey. What did you mean by me and my colleagues?"

He stopped. "I just spoke to your colleague from the Express and told him the exact same thing I'm telling you. We are working here, trying to solve a crime and we don't have anything to say this far, simply because we don't know much."

"Frederik?" I was surprised. They were never that fast at the Express to come out here. Most of the times they never cared much about what happened outside of Naestved, not enough to get out of their offices and actually come here. Plus it was a twenty minute drive. At least. That meant they had to have known much before I did. Even if they also had a police-scanner, they had to have heard it long before I did. How did they manage to do that?

Johannes Lindstroem shook his head. "No it was a new guy. A Lonstrom or something like that."

"Christian Lonstedt?"

Johannes Lindstroem snapped his fingers. "Yes. That was the name. Nice guy, not like that other one they usually send out. He was really pleasant company. Hope to see much more of him. Well gotta get back to work," he said and waved at me.

"I'll call later for details, then," I yelled back at him.

He waved back nodding. Then he disappeared back into the gymnasium and left me speechless on the pavement outside. I wasn't used to actually having competition.

I went around the building and found Sune. I paused when I saw that he was talking to someone. My heart dropped. It was him. That guy again. Christian Lonstedt. They were laughing. Why were they laughing? Why were they suddenly so familiar, like old friends?

I approached them. Christian Lonstedt was smiling showing pearly white teeth. His hair was impeccable. He was way too good looking to be nice, I thought. He already annoyed me. They both went quiet when I came closer.

"So what's so funny?" I asked.

Sune shook his head. "Nothing. Just a joke. It won't be as funny if repeated. It was a 'should have been there in the moment' kind of thing."

"Yeah. You really should," Christian said.

"You were here mighty early," I said to Christian. "How did you hear about it?"

Christian gave me one of his irresistible smiles. "Well that's not something I care to share with you. After all you do work for the competitor." He looked at me and shrugged. Then he tilted his head. "Sorry."

"It's okay. I wouldn't share it with you if it was me," I said.

"Scooped up anything good?" I asked Sune.

He nodded. "Got some pretty nice shots. Should make the old editor happy," he said and tapped his camera. "Got anything from the police? Any statements?"

I shook my head. "No. They won't talk. Not yet they say. I'll have to call him later."

"I think I might have gotten something," Christian said. "I know who it is. I know who was killed."

I froze. Johannes Lindstroem had told me that he hadn't told him anything. How did he get his information?

"How did you get that information?" Sune asked.

Christian smiled secretly again.

"He's not going to tell you that," I said. I pulled Sune's sweater. "Come on let's get back to the office. We have our own ways of finding out these kinds of things."

"Nice meeting you," Sune said addressed to Christian.

"Likewise," Christian said while nodding. "And you too Rebekka."

"So what did you do with Tobias today?" I asked while we walked back towards our cars.

Sune found his keys in his pocket. He didn't look at me when he spoke. "A neighbor took him for the day."

"You had a neighbor take care of him?"

Sune clicked the remote and unlocked his car. He shrugged while nodding. "Yes."

"Wow."

"What?"

"Nothing. I'm just a little surprised. That's all." I opened the door to my own car.

Sune exhaled. "So now you have an opinion on who I let take care of my kid as well. Is there anything you don't interfere in?"

"No. It's not like that. It's just that ..." I stopped myself. "You know what? You're right. It's none of my business anyway."

"That's right," Sune said.

I slammed the door to the car and walked towards him. "Come on," I said. "A neighbor? Really?"

"Please tell me what's wrong with that ..." Sune sighed.

"Why? Why would you rather place your son with a complete stranger than have him spend the day with his best friend in the whole world?"

"Just stay out of it," Sune said and got into his car.

I exhaled and gesticulated resigned with my arms. "Fine. Have it your way. Punish your son for no reason."

I slammed my hand against the steering wheel several times on the way back to the office cursing last night and the red wine. Sara was already in the editorial room.

"Thought you'd need a little extra help listening in on the police today," she said with a smile.

I was happy to see her. Mostly because that meant Sune and I didn't have to be alone all day. I needed him to stay and do a job for me and I really needed him to be in a good mood in order to persuade him to help me with this.

Sara had brought carrot cake. It was Sune's favorite and I brought him a piece from the kitchen along with a freshly brewed cup of coffee. He was in the middle of uploading the pictures taken this morning. He looked up from the screen. Our eyes locked and for a second it felt like before. He smiled quickly. I shrugged and ate some of my cake. He picked his up and started eating.

"So what do you want?" he asked.

"What? Can't I bring you coffee and cake without wanting something from you? Maybe I just want to thank you for being at the scene early on a Saturday morning. It was really great that you were able to react this fast."

"Still slower than the Express," he said. "That Christian guy was already there when I arrived. Can you believe that he does his own pictures? Some papers have started doing that, cutting out the photographer. Some journalists like Christian are trained to do both. Scary development. If it catches on I'll be out of work in a few years."

I nodded pensively. I understood his concern. It was something that newspapers had started doing a lot lately. Even the TV stations were training their reporters to make their own shoots so they didn't have to pay for a cameraman as well. VJs they called it. Photojournalists were also getting more and more common on my old newspaper, Jyllandsposten, the national paper I worked for before I moved back to Karrebaeksminde.

I shook my head. "Good photographers will always be in demand," I said.

"I sure hope so," Sune said while eating his cake.

"I'm sorry," I said. "I'm sorry for earlier. It really was none of my business."

Sune smiled shortly and nodded. "Well I'm sorry too." He paused and looked at me. "For everything. Today and yesterday."

"It's okay," I said. "Water under the bridge."

He nodded pensively. "So you never answered my question."

"What question?"

## Three, Four ... Better lock your door

"What did you want?" he asked and pointed at the half-eaten carrot cake.

"Oh. That. Well there is one thing I'd like to ask you to do for me ..."

"I knew it." Sune leaned back in his chair and smiled. "Bring it on."

"Well. You know how Christian said that he knew who the victim was?"

"Yes. And?"

"I really need to know that as well. I can't have him run the story before us. Jens-Ole will kill me. This is my story, this is our exclusive story. It has to stay that way. If the Express has some information that we don't then we need to find it. Maybe find it somewhere else than where they did. Maybe like somewhere we're not supposed to look."

Sune stopped smiling. "I think that I know where this is going and the answer is no. I can't risk it, Rebekka. If the police catch me hacking into their systems and files I'll be locked up for a long time. I have a record, you know."

"I know. I'm sorry," I said and walked back to my desk and sat down. "I shouldn't have asked. It was just stupid. We'll let Christian Lonstedt and his self-taught photographs win this round. We'll beat him next time, I'm sure."

Sune was growling behind his computer screen. I knew how much real photographers loathed these self-taught journalists who thought they could do as good a job as a real photographer could. People like Sune considered themselves artists who just happened to have to work for a newspaper to earn money, but they would never want to be compared to someone like Christian who didn't understand the beauty of photography the way people like Sune did. They didn't know how to use the light and the scene to create something beautiful even from something as dark and ugly as the scene of crime. Sune could do that. He was even brilliant at that.

Sune snorted and slammed his fist in the desk. "I'll do it," he said.

I looked at him with a smile.

"It went well last time, right?" he argued with his own conscience.

"It sure did. And I'll take all the blame if you're ever arrested again," I said. "I'll tell them that you did it on my order. Since you're afraid of being out of work soon because of the tough times being a photographer, you felt forced to do it. Because of your son, naturally. You need to feed your son, right?"

"Right," Sune growled. "But you're paying me double for this. I'll overcharge you for today."

"Sure." I jumped up from my chair and went to Sune's desk. "Here's the thing. I have been thinking. Someone had to have found the body this morning, and then called the police. They sent out a patrol to look into it since it might be just a prank or something else. The two officers first on the scene always leave a report when they get back and since it is past noon now they are definitely done with it. So I figured you could get me access to that report and then keep an eye out for the next one coming later today from the people working out there right now. Then I would like access to the forensics report of Susanne Larsen's death. They have to have that by now in the system. Then we can tell if the two cases are in any way connected."

## Chapter 14

It didn't take Sune more than a few minutes to hack his way into the police files. I watched him with excitement as his fingers danced across the keyboard. Sune was so talented at many things but this was really what he did best. Even if it was illegal, this was his element. There was no doubt.

"Got it," he said and leaned back with his arms behind his head. "It's amazing how bad they are at protecting themselves against attacks from the outside," he said.

I smiled and walked behind him. I leaned in over him on his chair to better see the screen. Being close to him again brought me back to the night before for a short second and caused something to stir inside of me. It was like we had opened a door we couldn't close again. I stepped back. I couldn't allow myself to act like this. I had to repress it.

Sune felt it too. He turned his head and looked up at me. I felt drawn to him and remembered how soft his lips had felt against mine. This was bad, I thought. This was really bad.

"Do you want to sit here while you read?" he asked and got up from his chair like he was in a hurry. He had blushed and his eyes avoided mine.

"Sure," I nodded.

"I'll just go out here, for a second," he said and pointed awkwardly at the door to the kitchen. "Get us some more coffee," he stuttered.

"You forgot the cups!" Sara yelled with a grin.

Sune returned. "It's okay. I'll take new ones."

"Bring me one as well," she said.

"Will do," he said and disappeared behind the door.

Sara stared at me.

"What?"

"Be very careful you two," she said while shaking her head.

I shook mine to pretend that I had no idea what she was talking about. Then I started scrolling through the police report from this morning. The call had come in at eight forty-seven. A guy named Brian Poulsen told them he worked weekends in the badminton club and had found a dead man in the men's dressing room when he went in to put up clean paper towels. The man was on the floor and there was blood all over the tiles even on the walls. "A bloodbath," he had called it. He had even been able to identify the victim, since it was his boss, the leader of the badminton club, Mr. Anders Hoejmark. The police officer had asked him over the phone to stay where he was while waiting for them and to not touch anything. But Brian Poulsen had not been there once the police had arrived.

So they would soon be starting a search for him, I thought. That meant they would need the media's help. Our newspaper was the strongest in this area and one that everybody around and in Karrebaeksminde read so they really needed our help to find this guy. That gave me an advantage. I was in a position where I could ask for something in return, such as some information that no one else had. I noted that on my pad.

I read through the rest of the report. The two officers sent to the sports center had arrived at five to nine and found the body in the shower. There was blood all over the tiles, they wrote. They had stayed clear of the scene and not touched anything. Then they called for backup and stayed at the scene until the forensic team arrived. They had then both consulted the police psychologist for an hour each.

I looked up from the screen. Why did they have to see a psychologist?

Sune returned from the kitchen with Sara's coffee and placed it at her desk. She smiled and thanked him. Then he retrieved our cups. He gave me mine in my hand. I drank while staring into thin air.

"Could you find the forensic report on Susanne Larsen?" I asked.

He sipped his coffee, then nodded. "Sure. Once I'm in there's really nothing much to it anymore."

I got up from his chair and as we passed each other our shoulders touched gently. His scent filled my nostrils and there it was again. That stir inside of me that feeling that I had no idea where to place was back. I glanced at Sara and saw her staring at us. I exhaled deeply and restrained myself. This had to stop. This longing, wanting to touch him, wanting to kiss him again. It had to be stopped before it went too far.

"Here it is," he said shortly after.

## Three, Four ... Better lock your door

This time I waited for him to move far away from the chair before I sat in it. I started scrolling slowly. When the pictures came up, my stomach turned. I literally felt like I was about to throw up. I held a hand across my mouth and fought the growing nausea. Sune came up behind me and looked at the screen as well.

"What the hell is that?" he exclaimed.

"Susanne Larsen I'm afraid. Or what's left of her at least."

I stared at the pictures once again. This time it wasn't as bad as the first, now that I was sort of prepared for it. Not that you'd ever be prepared for this kind of thing, this kind of cruelty. The first pictures were taken at the scene of crime. In the shower of what I assumed had to be the hotel room at the inn. Her arms seemed to be handcuffed to the faucet, to the pipe connecting the cold and warm. Her wrists were ripped to blood from trying to pull herself free, the forensics concluded. I shivered while I tried to imagine what must have gone through her mind while desperately fighting to pull her hands out.

Her body, especially her back was rippled with striped bruises that indicated she had been whipped with something similar to a leather belt, the report said. I swallowed hard as I watched her head closer. It looked like it had been cut open with a very sharp knife. A scalpel, the report stated. A very thin cut had been made just above the eyes and into the brain where the killer had cut off the connections to and from the prefrontal cortex, the anterior part of the frontal lobes of the brain. The incision had disconnected certain nerves in the brain and then the killer had left the victim to die from bleeding to death in the shower. The cut didn't seem professionally made, the report stated and the way the cut was made indicated - along with marks and bruises on her face and hands that the victim had still been alive and fully awake when the incision was made. She had probably passed out from the pain at some point before the incision was fully completed. If not the victim had to have lost her consciousness by the time the neural pathways were cut.

I leaned back in Sune's chair. He was behind me reading along with me. None of us were making a sound. I felt sick.

"What the hell is this?" he asked.

I exhaled deeply. "It looks like someone performed a lobotomy on Susanne Larsen while she was fully awake."

Sune turned and walked away for a second. He was twisting and turning, leaning over to catch his breath, gasping for air. "That's so sick, I can't believe it," he stuttered.

"My guess is the same thing happened to the dear president of the badminton club," I said heavily.

"Why do you say that?"

"Cause it stated in the report from this morning that the officers first on the scene had to see the police psychologist afterwards."

"Wow. Sounds like you could be right," Sune said. His face was so pale, even paler than usual.

"Plus he was also found in a shower."

"Reminds me of the movie *Psycho*," Sune said. "Seems like a pattern for the killer then?"

"Could very well be," I said. "Like a ritual."

"What does the report say about the killer? Do they have anything on him? Fingerprints, DNA?"

I scrolled to the long text underneath the pictures. "The handcuffs and the whipping and bruising and the fact that they had found semen inside of her indicates that she had been engaged maybe in some kind of S&M sex game with a man."

"Okay. Then they must have a DNA-profile?" Sune asked pensively.

"They do. But he's not in their system."

"Then it's no good," Sune exclaimed.

"Not now, but later. Plus if they find any DNA on the scene where Anders Hoejmark, the president of the badminton club was murdered then they'll at least know that it was the same guy."

"But Anders Hoejmark was a guy? Is the killer a sort of bi-sexual S&M monster?" Sune asked.

I shrugged. "Could be. Maybe he likes both. Maybe there's a reason. We have all the details we need and more. At least we can make the article about who it was that was killed this morning at the badminton club. As soon as the forensic report arrives we can also publish the article about the connection between the two killings."

"If they are," Sune stated.

"Of course. We also need to make sure that the victim's family has been informed before we run the identity of him. I'll call Johannes Lindstroem in a couple of hours to make sure. We want to be first with the story, but not at any cost. Not if the family isn't informed yet. I don't want them to learn about it in the online paper. That would be terrible."

I opened another file in the folder of Susanne Larsen and started reading the investigation report.

"Hmm," I said.

"What?" Sune came closer.

"Apparently Susanne Larsen led a sort of double-life."

"Well we kind of had that feeling already," Sune said. "That she had been having an affair with someone, right?"

"Yeah. But we never suspected this. I don't know about you, but I for one didn't."

## Three, Four ... Better lock your door

Sune came up behind me and looked at the screen again. "What do you mean? What didn't we suspect?"

"According to the police-investigation they found out that she had been chatting with several men over the computer lately and found lovers that she casually met with. She joined a sex-chat on the Internet that is strictly for people into hardcore S&M, you know one of these where you don't give them your real name and then you meet and have sex and never see each other again. That way you can keep it a secret and still have your weird desires satisfied."

"I get the picture," Sune said.

"It also says here that this information has to be kept from the press since her husband and children don't know," I continued.

"Protecting their own and the kids. Can't blame them, can we?"

"No, of course not. But it is interesting."

"How so?" Sune asked.

"It means that the police are looking for the guy she met up with, the guy she met through this website and they're also looking for this guy, Brian Poulsen."

Sune looked at me. "So now you want me to try and hack into Brian Poulsen's computer and find out if he is also into hardcore S&M and if he likes to chat with others, and meet up with others, who enjoy the same pleasures as he. And maybe - if we should only be so lucky - if he has been chatting with Susanne Larsen. Is that it?"

"Well I actually hadn't thought that far yet," I said grinning, "but since you mention it, then that sounds like a great idea. Could you do that? Could you find him?"

Sune pulled up another chair and pushed me aside so he could reach the computer. "I can certainly give it a try," he said.

I leaned back and sipped my coffee while watching the magician at work. I enjoyed that we were being a team again. It felt like we were suddenly back to normal. There was one thing I was going to make sure from now on, I decided. I was never going to let anything as stupid as a kiss come between us again. I couldn't afford for it to happen again.

No matter how badly I wanted it.

## Chapter 15

IT WAS HARDER THAN ANTICIPATED TO FIND THIS BRIAN POULSEN AND get into his computer. First of all because it was a pretty common name and just alone in Karrebaeksminde Sune found three people by that name. But second of all because Brian Poulsen himself - once Sune located who we believed to be the right one, the one that we found through the county's computers where it stated he had been ordered to take the job at the badminton club as a part of what they called an "Activation package" - turned out to be quite the computer nerd himself. He had put up a very difficult protection shield of some sort, that I didn't understand and Sune had a difficult time breaking through it. On top of that we were running out of time, since we were certain that soon the police were going to try and use the same angle as we did and they might just somehow "run into Sune" in cyberspace while he was trying to crack the codes as well. It made Sune sweat heavily and swear while he tried and tried again.

Meanwhile I started writing my article about this morning's homicide at the badminton club. When I had written the first few lines I picked up the phone and called Johannes Lindstroem. He confirmed that the deceased was Anders Hoejmark, the daily leader, or president of the club and that his family had been informed earlier in the day.

"How do you know this?" he then asked. "We haven't told a soul yet."

"Let's just say I have my sources," I answered.

"So does your friend at the *Express* apparently. That Frederik guy called me just a minute ago and told me they had already put it on their online paper. Can you believe that? Without having it confirmed by me first or even making sure that the family had been informed.

What a nerve they have. Could you have imagined what would have happened if we haven't found the family yet?"

"That would have been terrible," I said.

"They said they got it from an anonymous tip," Johannes Lindstroem continued.

So Christian had been lucky, I thought. Someone had tipped them. Maybe that was why he had been first at the scene. But who would know about the body other than the killer himself? Could Brian Poulsen have called the paper after he had found the body? Maybe to make a few extra bucks? They were known to pay their informers at the Express. Maybe that was why he hadn't stayed behind for the police to come? Either that or he was the killer of course.

"So do you have any suspects yet?" I asked Johannes Lindstroem.

"We would like to get a hold of Brian Poulsen, the young man who works at the badminton club in the weekends and who called the alarm central this morning and told us about the body. When the police arrived he was nowhere to be found."

"Do you consider him to be a suspect?"

"Not yet. But we would like to talk to him. It's very urgent."

"I'll make sure to write that," I said and wrote it on my notepad. "Do you have a picture of him somewhere we can print?"

"We're getting one ready as we speak. I'll make sure it's e-mailed to you so it can be in the morning paper. Make sure to state that he is not a suspect but that we want to talk to him as soon as possible."

"I'll make sure to do that. Then maybe you could give me something in return?" I knew I was stretching my good-will but I really needed something else to put in the article that the Express hadn't already told in their on-line paper.

Johannes Lindstroem sighed. "Like what?"

"I just need a comment on a few details. If you don't care to elaborate then just say yes or no."

"Very well, bring it on."

"I have a feeling the two killings - Susanne Larsen and Anders Hoejmark - are connected. Is that true?"

Johannes Lindstroem hesitated before he answered. "Yes. We believe they are. We don't know for sure. We haven't found any DNA at the second scene and no fingerprints at any of them that we can match. But as I said we still believe they are connected."

"Same modus operandi?"

"Both of them have been killed by the exact same procedure, yes."

I sighed with relief. This meant I could put it in my paper now that he had confirmed it and commented on it.

"Both killed in the shower? Both of them have been lobotomized?" I asked.

Johannes Lindstroem went quiet for a long time. "Where did you get that information from?" He said very seriously.

"I talked to someone - a source who shall remain nameless - who told me how Susanne Larsen had died, the rest I guessed," I lied. It sounded plausible.

"Very well. I cannot lie. Yes that is the case. Both bodies have been subjected to something that looks like a lobotomy."

"And then bled to death?"

"Yes."

"Were they both alive when it was done?"

He exhaled deeply. "I don't think people need this kind of detailing."

"Okay. I'll keep that out then."

"Good," he said relieved.

I went on. "Do we know if the killer is a male or female?"

"We're pretty sure it is a male."

"Why?"

"Because we found semen in the first victim and the second victim nearly strangled with one hand and held down even as he fought for his life. It looks like the job of a very strong man."

I nodded and noted eagerly. "The way the victims were killed, what does that tell you about the killer you're looking for?"

"He has to be one sick bastard."

I noted on my pad so fast it almost hurt my hand. This was a great and very strong statement.

"Is it fair to say that we have a serial-killer?" I asked.

"It might be."

"Is it or isn't it?"

"Well normally we say that a serial-killer is someone who murders more than three victims one at a time in a relatively short interval. That's the definition. So if we stick to that, then no."

"Not yet," I stated and wrote it down. "Are you expecting more killings in the future? Do you think he will kill again?"

"We always hope for the best and prepare for the worst. We sincerely hope to find this killer before he strikes again. It is after all very rare in Denmark that a murder mystery remains unsolved."

"You said you'd found semen, so that means you must have a DNA-profile?"

"We have a DNA-profile, yes. But haven't found a match yet."

I noted on my pad. More that I could now put in my article.

"Listen I really have to go now ..." he said.

"Just one more thing."

He paused. "Okay. One more."

"Should people in Karrebaeksminde be afraid?"

Johannes Lindstroem sighed deeply. He didn't answer for a long time. I knew this was a delicate question. At one point the police didn't want to scare the public on the other hand they didn't want any more victims. They wanted people to stay safe and be cautious.

"Okay. Let me rephrase that," I said. "Will you tell your own family to stay inside after sunset tonight?"

He inhaled deeply then exhaled while he spoke. "Yes. Yes I will."

"So people should be afraid?"

"I know I am."

## Chapter 16

I wrote three articles. One about the new killing, one about the search for Brian Poulsen and one about how the head of the police in Karrebaeksminde wants people to be careful. I put in all of Johannes Lindstroem's statements and then I sent everything to my editor feeling pretty good about it. This had to be a lot better than what the Express had been able to come up with.

I was right. Jens-Ole called me a few minutes later and was very pleased.

"I loved the part where he says that 'It has to be one sick bastard' that's excellent. Scary too. I'm not much into scaring our readers, but I think he is right. We need to be careful these days with a guy like him on the loose. Lobotomy? Who would come up with such a creepy thing?"

"I don't know," I said and stared at Sune. He was still working at trying to gain access to Brian Poulsen's computer. Apparently he really had his work cut out for him on this. But Sune wasn't the type who just gave up, I was pleased to see.

"Sure would make a great horror movie," Jens-Ole said. "I want you to do an article about lobotomy for tomorrow. We need to keep this story going. This is our story now, this is yours. We need some more insight. What is lobotomy exactly? Where was it used and so on? Enlighten people a little."

I noted his idea. "I'll get on it right away," I said and hung up. I turned and looked at Sara. She took off her headphones. "Any news?" I asked.

She shook her head. "They're closing everything down now at the sports center. They're done."

"Could I ask you to help me on some research?" I asked.

## Three, Four ... Better lock your door

"Sure."

"I want to write a story about lobotomy. Could you find some articles and an expert who would want to do an interview tomorrow morning?"

"With pleasure," she said and started typing.

I received an e-mail, the picture of Brian Poulsen that the police had sent me. I forwarded it to my editor along with Sune's pictures from the same morning. We didn't have a picture of the body leaving the scene this time but what we had was also great. Sune had done an excellent job. The pictures of the forensic team working were splendid, almost beautiful. The way he used the light and the shadows made it almost artistic and less nauseating. The detailing was perfect. He had captured how they worked with tweezers and small brushes marvelously. I was very proud to send it all to my editor.

After it was done I went to the kitchen and brought back more coffee for Sune and Sara. They were both working so hard on making me look good. I was truly grateful.

I sat behind my desk and started researching a little myself on lobotomy and its use. According to Wikipedia Lobotomy was a neurosurgical procedure that was controversial since its inception in 1935, it became a mainstream procedure for more than two decades, prescribed for psychiatric - and occasionally other - conditions despite the recognition of serious side-effects.

The idea was that the procedure was supposed to attenuate the anxiety and unrest the patient was feeling, but many patients became almost apathetic. The nerves were destroyed and many patients ended up as vegetables and lots of them died. In 1946 a man named Walter Freeman took an ice pick from his own kitchen and hit it through the forehead of a patient just above the eyeballs and managed to cut over the nerve paths and thereby invented a new way of doing the lobotomy - a way he later used with a scalpel on more than two-thousand four hundred patients. Some of his operations were even shown on TV in the United States. From the early 1940's until the mid-1950's it was commonly used on psychiatric patients until modern antipsychotics were introduced. By 1951 almost twenty thousand lobotomies had been performed in the United States. After that it was slowly phased out over there. But apparently not in Denmark.

Denmark was an ugly statistic when it came to the use of lobotomy. Denmark had the world record for the most lobotomies compared to the size of the population and the usage of the procedure continued way into the 1990's according to a website I found. Someone, a historian, recently wrote a book about his discovery and was interviewed by a paper, but I couldn't seem to find the article in the paper's database. The article was mentioned on this website where they quoted from it. According to what they wrote, the historian stated that "many Danes were lobotomized between 1947 and 1993, and many died from the operation. Doctors did not count on curing them completely, but wanted to pacify them, perhaps to better their condition."

I leaned back a little shocked. Was this really true? Had they done that this late? In the nineties? The article was only two years old, but I had never heard of this before, nor had I heard about the book.

"I think I might have found someone," Sara said.

I looked at her.

"You probably know her already. She's pretty famous. Dr. Irene Hoeg. She's the Chief Psychiatrist at Rigshospitalet, Copenhagen's University Hospital."

"Also known as the leader of the political right-wing populist party 'Danish Front,'" I said. "She's the one with the most nationalistic opinions. Never afraid to say just what she means. Always a spokeswoman for the 'Let's get rid of all the immigrants and anyone who doesn't look anything like us' -opinion that is growing in this country."

Sara nodded. "I've seen her in the news." She paused. "She has also won prizes for her research on the human brain. She agreed to tell you about lobotomy. She is an expert on the subject, the best in the country. But you'll have to drive to Copenhagen early in the morning. She has agreed to meet you at her house at ten even though it is Sunday."

"Good work everyone," I said. "Let's call it a day."

Sune stared at me with disbelief. "I'm not done yet," he groaned.

"Let's leave it and try again tomorrow. Maybe the police will do the work for us. Then we can read about it in the report."

Julie gave me an angry look when I entered the door to my father's house. It was almost dinner time and Dad was in the kitchen. Julie was sitting by the table still with the game of monopoly in front of her.

"Smells great, Dad," I said and threw my bag on a chair.

"You're right on time," he said. "Dinner is ready in five."

I grabbed a chair and sat next to Julie. "Sorry I had to leave you like that, sweetie," I said.

"Why didn't Tobias come here today? Wasn't Sune at work with you?" she asked.

I sighed. "Yes he was. But Sune had a neighbor watch him."

Julie wrinkled her small nose. "But why?"

I shrugged. A bowl of steaming potatoes landed on the table in front of me. I started packing the game back in its package to make room for the food and plates. "Who knows? Maybe the neighbor wanted to play with him? Maybe they're friends?"

"Tobias doesn't have any other friends. He told me that." Julie snorted.

I put my hand to cover hers. "I know you want to play with him, and I'm sure he will be back someday soon. But Tobias and Sune have other things too. We're not the only people in their lives."

Julie snorted. "I think you screwed it up. You did something. I just know you did. You ruined everything."

A dish with lamb chops landed on the table. It smelled incredible. I looked at Julie. She was almost in tears. I didn't know what to say to her. Even if Sune and I were still friends we had to keep apart socially for a while. It was crucial that we did. I really didn't want to separate the children because of it but it was hard to see any alternatives. Dad sat down. He looked at us both.

"Let's eat."

## Chapter 17

Dr. Irene Hoeg looked like she always did on TV. She wore her long hair in a bun on the neck and a tight strict smile making her seem superior to others. She was wearing a white shirt and nice beige pants with creases. She was in her mid-sixties but looked much younger. Her skin was light, her eyes blue and her hair dyed blond. She was tall for a woman I noticed as I entered her huge mansion in Hellerup north of Copenhagen - the whiskey belt as it was called since so many rich people lived there. Her handshake was firm and strong. It almost hurt my fingers.

She showed me into her office and sat behind a huge mahogany desk. I sat in a chair in front of her quite intimidating desk.

"Can I get you anything?" she asked. "Coffee?" She pointed at a tray next to us with two cups and a silver pot.

"That would be nice. It was a long drive."

"Help yourself," she said.

I poured a cup and put in some milk. I sipped it while finding my notes. I looked up. Behind Irene were framed pictures of her and people she had worked with in front of different buildings. She noticed I was looking at the pictures.

"Yes after more than thirty years in psychiatry I have been around," she stated. "I began my career at Montebello in Elsinore."

"The psychiatric hospital that was later made into an asylum camp for refugees from the war in ex-Yugoslavia, right?"

"Yes and now I believe it is a nursing home for the elderly among other things. Back in the old days it was called a Sanatorium. Where people with bad nerves were admitted. In 1969 a youth section was created at Montebello. That was where I started my career as a psychiatrist."

# Three, Four ... Better lock your door

"When was that?"

"1975. I worked with young people for many years. It wasn't until 2001 when I was headhunted to the position at Rigshospitalet that I stopped working with the youngsters."

"Did they do lobotomies at Montebello?"

She nodded. "They did. But only in very rare and difficult cases where there was no other treatment that would work. It stopped shortly after I had started working there. In 1977 they did the last one."

"Have you ever done any?"

"I actually performed the last one in Montebello. After that the politicians decided to stop it. It was my first and my last."

I nodded and noted it. So she did really know what she was talking about. She hadn't only read about it in textbooks in med-school. That was good. Scary, but good.

"So what can you tell me about lobotomy? How did you feel about having to do that procedure on someone?"

"The patient was no more than eighteen years old. She had severe manic-depression and paranoia and there was nothing more we could do for her. We had given her electro-shock, held her down in a straitjacket; we had strapped her down, everything you did back then to help a young woman in her situation. But she kept hurting herself. She tried to kill herself and even others who came near her at times. She was just dangerous to her surroundings and in the end, once you've tried all there is to try; you go for the last resort. I recommended the lobotomy after consulting the other doctors at the facility and we all agreed on doing this. It really was the best for everybody."

"So what happened to her afterwards?"

"She lived the rest of her life in a nursing home, died ten years ago, I believe. The point is that it actually worked for her. I know it's controversial but the fact remains that it did help some patients back in those days."

"But didn't you ever think that it was a little excessive to open a person's brain and cut the nerve paths?"

Irene Hoeg shook her head. "We didn't back then. The idea was to cut off the connection in the brain so to speak, it was believed that thoughts and ideas and patterns were stored in the nerves of the brain. Insanity was a thought process that was kept in the nerve paths and if you cut those you could remove bad or abnormal thinking and behavior. It was a clinical procedure along with so many others. All I ever saw was that it worked."

"But it also killed a lot of patients by damaging their brains and others became apathetic vegetables for the rest of their lives. Like your patient who ended up in a nursing home," I said.

"Correct. But wasn't that better than her killing someone? That was what she was going to do. She was a wild beast. I do believe we saved her from doing something really bad either to herself or to others."

I noted on my pad while thinking that I understood what she was saying but couldn't escape the thought that there had to have been some other way to treat the poor girl.

"But today we luckily have antidepressants and antipsychotics," I said.

The doctor closed her eyes and nodded slowly. "That we do."

"The article that I'm doing is sort of a background story about lobotomy. You know its history, who invented it, where was it used in Denmark and so on. But what I really would love to add to the article is a little detailed information about the procedure itself."

Dr. Irene Hoeg leaned over her desk. "Like what?"

"You have tried it, right?" I said.

The doctor nodded. "Like I told you. Once." She lifted her forefinger to emphasize that it was only the one time.

"Is it difficult?"

The doctor looked at me with wonder. "Is what difficult?"

"To make the cut precisely. Is it something anyone can do?"

Dr. Irene Hoeg remained pensive for a few seconds. "I don't believe anyone could do it correctly, no. You need to know about the brain. How it is put together, where everything is at, where to open it, which nerves to cut."

"Of course, but if the purpose is to kill someone, then it's not that hard is it?"

"I suppose not. If you don't care what you do then no. Anyone with a scalpel can open up the brain and cut the nerves. Provided that they know how to hold and cut with a scalpel of course."

I speculated as I wrote on my pad. The forensic report had stated that it didn't seem like a professional cut, but also that it was hard to tell since Susanne Larsen had still been alive and therefore had tried to fight for her life. Could it have been professionally made if she hadn't moved and fought? I looked at Dr. Irene Hoeg's hands. They were shaking slightly. Could the cut have been made from someone who used to do this professionally but now was older? But how was the murderer then supposed to be so physically superior to Anders Hoejmark that he could hold him with only one hand? Maybe if he was strong and in shape like Dr. Hoeg, despite her age? It was possible. Somehow this had to have a connection to what had been done back then. Somehow the killer was trying to state something by performing this procedure on his victims. But why? What kind of statement was it? Why was it so important?

"I think that was everything," I said and got up from my chair.

## Three, Four ... Better lock your door

"That was fast," Dr. Hoeg said and escorted me to the front door. She walked with strong athletic movements.

As we reached the door I turned and looked at her. "Say have you heard about the historian who wrote a book two years ago stating that there had been cases of use of lobotomy on patients in the Nineties?"

Irene Hoeg shook her head. "I know of this so-called medical historian and his work. It's not true. The lobotomies ended in the late Seventies in this country. Of that I am certain. No psychiatric patients have been lobotomized since."

"But where did he get his information from then?"

"I don't know where he gets his ideas from. It's ludicrous. But I do know that he was forced by the publisher right after the publication of the book to recall it and excuse all of his statements made in it. It was merely accusations. He was just trying to get his fifteen minutes of fame. Now if you'll excuse me I have a granddaughter to see. It's her birthday."

"It was very kind of you to see me today," I said and shook her hand one more time before I walked down the stairs. The gravel crunched under my feet as I walked across the driveway to my car.

I had a strange feeling as I turned on the engine, a feeling that I needed to find this medical historian and talk to him.

## Chapter 18

Back at the office I wrote an article on 'The history of lobotomy through times' and another one about how it was used in Denmark. I didn't get into the discussion about when it had stopped in Denmark. Instead, I used Irene Hoeg's statement that she had done the last one at the psychiatric hospital where she was back then and that she had no knowledge of there being done any more after that.

"I'm in!" I heard Sune exclaim. "I am finally in!"

I looked up from the screen and my eyes met his. He had both his arms over his head. "I did it," he said.

I grabbed my coffee cup and walked towards his desk.

"I did what the police have been trying to do since yesterday," he said.

"What do you mean?"

"They have the computer. When I got in this morning I realized that it had been moved. But I localized it as soon as they turned it on. I had a feeling they would search Brian Poulsen's apartment at some point and take his computer with them, so I put in a small tracking device in the server. This morning when they turned it on they couldn't get in. He has the best protection on it that I've ever seen. I'm pretty amazed by it. But nevertheless when they turned it on I was able to get access through what I like to call a back-door."

I stared at Sune. I had no idea what he was talking about. I just nodded along and hoped it would make sense at some point.

"Anyway," he said. "I'm not going to bother you with details on how I did it, but just let you know how awesome I am. Now I can find out everything about this guy, everything he has been up to and

## Three, Four ... Better lock your door

maybe why he has been so busy protecting himself from attacks from the outside. Now what are you hiding?" he asked the screen.

"Just let me know if you find anything," I said and went for more coffee in the kitchen. There was no cake today since Sara had stayed home, but right at that moment I felt so hungry for it. It was funny how the body got used to having its daily sugar kick. It was like a drug really. I stared at the street beneath me. It was empty. All the tourists and locals that normally filled the streets in a great weather like this were completely evaporated. My articles the same morning about the lobotomy-killer had done this. People were staying inside now. Tourists were fleeing the town, boats had left from the marina and everywhere there normally was so much life at this season was now empty and vacant. I felt sad for having been the one to make this happen. But I was after all just the messenger. It just seemed so sad. It started to rain as I stared at the buildings in front of me. A silent dusty rain fell slowly from the sky above.

Just at that second I spotted someone walking towards our building. He had drawn the hood from his sweater over his head, still I recognized him. My heart dropped. It was Christian Lonstedt. What was he doing here?

I walked to the editorial room and heard his steps on the stairs outside. The door handle turned and his head peeked in. He smiled his dazzling smile.

"Mr. Express!" Sune exclaimed and got up from the chair. "Come on in."

"Am I interrupting anything?" Christian asked.

"No. Just the usual work, you know," Sune said and they made some sort of street-smart handshake. "To what do we owe the honor?"

Christian took down the hood and shivered slightly from the cold. "Nothing. Was just in the neighborhood and wanted to say hi."

I put down my cup of coffee on the desk next to me. "Really?" I said. "That was nice of you. What are you doing all the way out here on a Sunday?"

"Oh I have the day off. No I was here on personal business and just thought I'd come up and congratulate you."

He looked at me kind of examining. I blushed to my own surprise. Why did I do that all of sudden. Why did I feel so self-conscious all of a sudden? This guy annoyed me. Why did I act like a school girl around him?

"Congratulate me on what?" I asked.

"Your articles in today's paper. They were really good. Much better than what we at the *Express* managed to do with it."

I was a little startled. Was he giving me a compliment and at the same time talking bad about his own work? I shrugged. "Well thank you. That was nice of you." I felt awkward as a silence occurred between the three of us. "Coffee?" I asked.

"Sure. That would be nice," Christian said.

"Grab a chair," I said and went to get all three of us some coffee. "I'm afraid we don't have any cake today," I said as I returned with three cups of hot coffee in my hands trying hard not to spill. "Usually we always have cake but Sara's not here today so ..."

I handed the cup to Christian and he took it. "It's perfectly fine," he said smiling. "Just the coffee is all that I need right now."

I pulled out a chair and sat in front of him while we sipped our coffee. I was beginning to think that I had misjudged the guy. I had taken him for being one of those smart ass clever fast paced journalists who just wanted their name in the paper at any cost. I was beginning to think that it wasn't him but the paper he was working for.

"So how do you enjoy working at the *Express*?" I asked.

"It's okay, I guess. It's work. Pays the bills."

"Where did you work before?" Sune asked.

"I actually just returned from Zimbabwe. I worked three years for Danida writing their press releases and web page and so on. Then I helped them out where I could in their charity work. You know fed villages and helped them build schools. That kind of stuff."

I swallowed hard. Okay the guy was a saint. And I had taken him for the devil. I felt bad.

"So how on earth did you end up on a paper like the *Express*?" I asked.

"Well I had one really bad experience while down there. An entire village was burnt to the ground while we were there. The villagers fled to the local church thinking that no one would burn down God's own house, but they did. The attackers blocked the entrance and set it on fire. They made us watch while they did it. To make us understand that anything we did in this country was in vain. We might as well go home, they said. We couldn't change Africa. We heard them burn alive inside of that church. Women, children and we knew every one of them. I especially had gotten to know a small boy who I had thought about trying to adopt and bring with me back to Denmark. He died in there as well. It was really terrible." Christian paused like he needed to shake the experience once again. "So that's why I left. We all did. Went back home. It took me a year in therapy to move on from this. I guess I just took the job I could get. To me it's more about getting out there and working again. Getting back on the horse as we say," he said with a smile and a shy shrug.

"Wow," I said. "That's some story."

"One of those that needs something stronger than coffee, Sune said and got up from his chair. He went to his desk and opened the bottom drawer. He pulled out a bottle of Aalborg Akvavit - Danish schnapps - and three shot-glasses. He put them on the table and poured schnapps in them while I was trying to digest that horrible story. It had really shocked me. Christian had surprised me; he was not at all the guy I took him for.

"Cheers," Sune said and lifted the glass.

"Cheers," Christian and I repeated. Our eyes locked as our glasses touched in the air. I felt a strange sensation. Like he was seeing right through me and I blushed again.

"To friends," Christian said.

"And good colleagues," Sune said. He had noticed how Christian and I were looking at each other, I could tell by the expression on his face. It was like he was frozen in a smile. I avoided looking into his eyes.

"Good colleagues," I repeated and emptied my glass. A warm sensation flowed through my veins.

"Well. I'd better be going now," Christian said and got up from the chair. "It's a nice little place you have here."

"I bet it's not as nice as the editorial room at the *Express*," Sune said.

Christian put his hood back on to cover his head. It was raining harder now. "Well it's a lot cozier, I tell you that." He turned and looked at me with warmth in his eyes. "So is the company," he said and nodded in my direction. "See you around."

## Chapter 19

Fat Linda was - as her nickname strongly implied - fat. She knew it and everybody else knew it. She hadn't always been like this though, she thought as she leaned back in her recliner that she could hardly fit into anymore. She picked up the second bag of chips today and grabbed out a handful that she dipped in ice-cream before they ended their day with the rest - crushed between her teeth then devoured and flushed down with liters of soda.

No, once Fat Linda Nielsen had been a normal girl, a young woman of a normal size and proportion. She had even been a happy young woman back then.

Linda chewed and channel-surfed the TV while trying hard not to think about that time. But it was hard not to.

She had been a nurse. A really good nurse once. The patients had liked her. She had helped them, talked to them and she had liked it. She liked that someone needed her and wanted her. It felt good to be needed.

Now she was stuck to this stupid chair all day reduced to this huge enormous creature that could hardly move. That hardly bothered to move anymore.

Fat Linda sighed and put the remote down. She stared at her lumpy legs underneath the bags of chips and pizza boxes. How had she ever ended up like this? She could hardly recognize herself any longer. These weren't her legs. How could they be? They looked nothing like those long tanned slim legs she had shown every summer riding her bike through town. They used to be her finest feature and cause all men to turn and stare at her. Now they were white and clumpy and made her waddle when she walked.

Why she had ended up like this, she wasn't sure. But it had

## Three, Four ... Better lock your door

started many years ago. Twenty years ago to be exact. She still remembered it vividly. The craving had come like a pulse from inside. Whenever she had thought about ... whenever she had thought about what she had done. That was when the longing for comfort had started. She had suddenly begun overeating, just stuffing her face with whatever was in the fridge or the cabinets. Then she went out to buy more to eat in front of the TV, alone while crying. The crying would make her eat even more. She would eat till she couldn't feel the desire to cry anymore, till she felt nothing at all, only the wonderful peaceful sensation of complete numbness. That was the fix she was looking for when she ate: to be utterly emotionless.

She only wanted all the unhealthy stuff. It was never carrots or apples or just normal food that she craved. It was only the greasy stuff, the things packed with sugar or fat that would comfort her. It did make her feel better - at least for a little while. Then the craving would return and she would start all over.

It had only taken her a few months to get really fat. Then she had lost her job and soon the ability to work at all. Now she received welfare from the state. It wasn't much, just enough to pay for her enormous consumption. Now she never had to move except to go shopping for more food every now and then. That was the worst part, the getting up, walking all the way, the stares and little children pointing their fingers at her. Linda knew she was a monster in their eyes and she loathed herself just as much as they did.

Fat Linda turned off the TV and exhaled. Even bathing had become quite the challenge. But it had to be done, and Fat Linda had started smelling from between the rapidly growing folds of flesh on her body. There were places she wasn't even able to reach anymore. Her social-worker had realized that it was a problem and signed her up for help. Now they sent some guy every week to give her a bath. It was embarrassing for Fat Linda not to be able to take care of herself anymore at the age of only forty-six. But she didn't know how to reverse things. She didn't know how to get back to real life. She didn't even know if she wanted to anymore. She had been away too long and it was too late for her. Besides, you couldn't reverse things done in the past. That much she knew, she thought as there was a knock on the door.

Fat Linda never even bothered to lock the door anymore, since it had become so hard to get up from her chair lately. Now she left it open so the pizza delivery guy could just walk right in and place her food on the table.

"Come on in," she yelled.

The handle turned and the door opened slowly. A face appeared. He was smiling. Fat Linda smiled back. Even if bathing had become a problem for Fat Linda, she truly enjoyed her new friend that the social worker had sent to help her out.

"Ready for your bath?" he asked and walked closer.

Fat Linda nodded and reached out her hand. "If you could just ..."

The man stepped closer and grabbed her hand. A shiver went through her body. She hadn't been with a man in many years.

He strained himself as he pulled her arms and helped her get out of the chair. Then he helped her waddle out to the bathroom.

## Chapter 20

FAT LINDA REALLY LIKED SVEND, MAYBE EVEN SO MUCH THAT THE thought to stop overeating for his sake went through her mind as he undressed her. He pulled her shapeless dress over her head and then he pulled off her bra and panties. He was always so gentle with her and made sure she was comfortable. What she liked the most about him was that he never seemed to dislike her or what she looked like. He didn't look at her with disgust like she was used to. He even smiled when he saw her naked and it sometimes made her blush. He made her feel things she hadn't felt in years.

The water was running in the bathtub filling it up. Svend had put in bubbles for her and bath salts to make her feel good. He held her hand to support her and helped her to slowly sink into the hot bubbly water.

Fat Linda closed her eyes and exhaled deeply as the water covered her huge body and made it feel light for once, like she was much smaller than she really was. Her knees ached from carrying all that extra weight and her heart was racing in her chest from merely moving, but it was only for a few seconds more. The bath would calm her body down.

Svend had brought a couple of red candles that he now lit and then shut off the light in the bathroom.

"There you go. This is much nicer," he said. "Enjoying it?"

"Mmm," she nodded with her eyes closed.

In her mind she was twenty-five again and she had just met Jonathan. He was tall and handsome and he liked her. He took her dancing, he took her to expensive restaurants and he met her parents. They took bicycle rides and picnicked in the forest. They laughed and enjoyed each other's company immensely. Jonathan was the love of Fat Linda's life. The one and only love she had ever encountered.

Fat Linda opened her eyes as Svend started washing her body with a washcloth. It felt so good, but at the same time she was extremely embarrassed as she felt him lift her folds of flesh to wash underneath them. She felt a pinch in her stomach when she realized that his hand almost disappeared under her skin. Like it was swallowed by her fatty lumps. She closed her eyes again and leaned her head back. Oh how she loathed herself and what she had become. But she could not go back. She could never be who she used to be. No Fat Linda had chosen this life for herself and now she had to live it until her body couldn't sustain it any longer, till it gave up. She deserved it for what she had done. It was only just.

"There, you're all clean," Svend interrupted her chain of thoughts.

Fat Linda opened her eyes. Svend smiled. It was a smile of mercy and pity, not love.

He doesn't like you; she heard that small thin voice in her mind say. Nobody does. Nobody ever will. You're not worth loving. Not anymore. You never will be again.

Fat Linda exhaled and watched Svend as he pulled out something from his bag. It was a book. He smiled politely as he sat on a chair next to her. She was just another job to him. Another pathetic patient who needed his help. Fat Linda knew that better than anybody. She had been like him when she had been a nurse. She had smiled the same way to her patients and let them know that they were liked and that she wasn't disgusted by them. She spoke in a nice tone of voice and made them believe she really cared about them. But she didn't. How could she? Who could care about someone like them? Nobody wanted them. Still they hadn't deserved what they had done to them.

"What are you reading?" Fat Linda asked.

Svend smiled again. "It's called *Under the burning sun*," he said. "It's really good."

Fat Linda smiled and nodded. She used to read, she loved reading. Romance novels mostly. Maybe it would bring her some joy back in her life if she tried to read again? The thought of once again escaping into different worlds and becoming different people intrigued her immensely. She needed the escape. The food just didn't do it for her any longer. Not like it used to.

"If you'd like I could get you some books from the library next time I come," Svend said as if he had read her mind.

"I'd like that a lot," Fat Linda said feeling a warmth rise inside of her by his kindness.

Svend looked at his watch. Then he got up from the chair. "You know what? I've totally lost track of time. I'd better get you up now. I have another patient that I have to be with in five minutes. I'm so sorry but you know we don't have long between visits in Home Care. Here let me take your hand and help you up."

Fat Linda sighed. She was really enjoying soaking in the hot water. It was such a nice change from just sitting and eating and watching TV.

Svend tilted his head. "Are you coming?" he said.

Fat Linda shook her head. "No. I want to stay. Go ahead and see your other patients, I'll get out on my own."

Svend looked at her with disbelief.

"It's okay, damn it," she said. "I'm forty-six years old. I should be able to get out of my bath on my own. You've done what you needed to do. You've washed me in places I can't reach. Now I want to do this on my own. I know I can. I don't want to be helpless for the rest of my life. I want to be able to do stuff on my own. I want to get out of this huge body that I don't even recognize anymore. I want to get back to who I used to be. I want to get better."

Fat Linda was crying now.

Svend kneeled next to her and held her hand. "You have no idea how excited I am to hear that," he said. "I'll tell Louise, your social worker, and let her know that you're ready to move on with your life." He patted her voluptuous arm gently. "This is really good, Linda. You have an entire life ahead of you, and you should be able to enjoy it."

"Now just leave me alone," she said sobbing.

"Are you sure? I still have a few minutes left."

"Just go. I'm fine. I want to do this."

Svend hesitated. Then he got up. "As you wish," he said.

He grabbed his backpack from the floor and swung it over his shoulder. "See you next Sunday, then?"

Fat Linda nodded and Svend left her in the bathtub. She felt at once humiliated and liberated. It had to stop now; she thought and stared down at her body. The bubbles were gone and now she saw the brutal reality of her own oversized flesh. It was time for a change. It was now or never.

Fat Linda closed her eyes one last time before she would try and get out of the tub on her own. She was gathering her strength thinking about herself losing all that weight and being able to do even ordinary things like go for a walk or maybe even ride on her bike again? She opened her eyes and smiled at the thought. Could she have a normal life again? Was it possible? Had she suffered long enough to finally be forgiven?

Maybe she had, she thought as her eyes glanced upon someone standing in the bathroom. A woman, dressed in a sparkling blue evening gown. Fat Linda's heart dropped. Those eyes, she thought to herself. She had seen them before. She had seen them in that operating room staring at her. Those were the eyes she had tried so hard to forget all of those years.

When the woman came closer and lifted the scalpel Fat Linda suddenly remembered everything. She relived it like a flash in her mind. The pain, the torment of knowing.

She also knew that she was going to die.

"I know why you're here," Fat Linda whispered with a shivering voice. Then she felt the sensation of plastic from the gloves around her neck holding her down while the scalpel came closer to her eyes.

Blood soon colored the bathwater and not long after Fat Linda finally reached her goal of twenty years. She became numb and would never feel anything again.

## Chapter 21

ABDUL HUSSEIN HATED TO DELIVER PIZZAS. HE HATED EVERYTHING about it. The driving around on his small scooter with all the stickers advertising "Pizza Mamma Mia", the stench from the boxes that was always in his clothes and hair, the customers who were always dissatisfied and thought he was too late, too slow and too stupid. The remarks, the scolding and yelling, the old women trying to seduce him. He loathed everything about it. He especially hated his father for forcing him to work every day after school and every weekend when Abdul would much rather hang out with his friends and go to the arcade or look at girls at the marina. Abdul really wanted a life like all of his Danish friends, but his father never understood that.

"When I was your age I worked at my dad's farm every day. I didn't even have the privilege of going to school," he said.

Abdul wanted to tell him that that was in another time in another country. A country Abdul felt in no way connected to anymore not since they fled and moved to Denmark to begin a new life in this cold but secure part of the world. Times change, he wanted to tell him. But how could he? After all his father had gone through to create a new life for them here? He gave up being a doctor for the safety of his family and moved to this country where his papers and diplomas were worth nothing, a country that had kept them in a camp for seven years before they had given them permission to finally move into their own apartment. His father who opened a pizzeria and worked all hours of the day to support his family. How could Abdul say no to him when he asked him for a little help every afternoon? Abdul would never do that. Delivering pizzas was something he had to do even if his Danish friends didn't understand. They told him to just say no to his father and come with them to drink beer in the marina or behind the Youth Club and then trash the place later when they were wasted enough.

Abdul had obligations. He had a family that depended on him. He couldn't let them down like that. Even if he sometimes wanted to.

Abdul Hussein thought about just taking off sometimes when he drove on his scooter with the stinking pizzas on the back. He was considering the possibility again on this day when he rode through the darkness while the cold rain hit his face. He could just keep going. They wouldn't know until later tonight when they realized that he hadn't returned. They would be worried, of course, especially his mother. They would call him on his cell phone but he wouldn't pick it up. Maybe he would even throw it away so they couldn't track him down. Then he would just keep going. Out of Karrebaeksminde, out on the long lonely roads leading to the vast country with only fields and cows and a farm now and then. He would keep going to see how far his scooter could take him. He could sleep in a barn and then just go on from there. Walk, when he ran out of gas. Just keep going. Where to, he didn't care. Just away from here. Away from this small town, away from his parents, away from the work, away from school where they always treated him like an imbecile even though he was better than most kids at math, the teachers just assumed he didn't understand because he had an accent when he spoke. All he wanted was to get away - and to never see a pizza again.

Abdul Hussein laughed as he turned the scooter into a small community of townhouses that the city had build for elderly and severely handicapped people. They were cheap houses to live in because the city paid some of the rent, someone had told Abdul once. He didn't understand where the Danish government got all the money from to take such good care of its citizens but he did know that the houses were much nicer than anything he had ever seen in his home country Syria and he also knew that he wouldn't mind living there and having the city pay some of his rent. But it was only for disabled or old people, he had been told.

Abdul came there a lot since he had a pretty steady customer who sometimes ordered in several times a day. From what he knew about her she was neither old nor disabled. In Abdul Hussein's old country they would have simply called her lazy. All he knew about her was that she sat all day and just ate in her big chair in the living room. She didn't even care to get up when he arrived any more. She just left the door unlocked so he could go right in. He always knocked first though. He was scared to death of one day finding her naked.

Abdul Hussein took the two pizzas she had ordered and brought them to the door. Then he knocked just before he opened the door.

"Miss Linda?" he said and went in even if she didn't answer. Probably just asleep, he thought and put the pizzas on the table next to her recliner. He turned and was just about to walk out, when he saw the water red as blood leaking from under the door to the bathroom. Abdul Hussein's heart started racing as he walked closer and pushed the door open.

Abdul Hussein really hated delivering pizza for all kinds of reasons but what he saw on the other side of the door made him realize that he was never going to be able to deliver another one again.

.

## Chapter 22

"I WANT TO FIND THAT MEDICAL HISTORIAN AND TALK TO HIM," I SAID. "I really think there is a huge story hidden in this somewhere."

It was still Sunday evening and I was arguing with my editor Jens-Ole on the phone. He wanted me to keep on the lobotomy murder case the next couple of days and try and find Brian Poulsen and talk to him instead.

"I know it's not easy, but think about it," he said. "Think if we could get an eye-witness description of what he saw in the shower at the club."

"But the police are looking for him too and they don't seem to be able to track him down so how do you suppose I should do that?" I said.

"I don't know, honey. That's why I pay you those big bucks to be my star reporter," he said.

"But I really want to pursue this other lead I have. Dr. Irene Hoeg is hiding something. There was something she was withholding for me, I could tell. I want to know what made him take back the book."

"Maybe it was a hoax. What do we care? It's just a man with a stupid book. I need something slightly more alive, something people can relate to, people in our area."

"I know, but I just think that there is something bigger there. I can't say what it is, it's just a feeling," I said.

"I'm sorry," Jens-Ole said. "A feeling doesn't sell newspapers. Nor does it give me an article I can put on the front page. I can't have you waste time on this. What about finding the first guy, the one who found Susanne Larsen's body? That should be easier."

I exhaled. "All right. I'll come up with something for you."

"Great. Can't wait to see it."

## Three, Four ... Better lock your door

Jens-Ole hung up. I looked at Sune. He was messing around in Brian Poulsen's computer. So far he hadn't found anything connecting him to Susanne Larsen. No visits to S&M sex-pages or chats with strangers. Not so far. I still wanted Sune to continue. If there was something in there we could use, I wanted to be the first to know. I turned my head and stared at Sara who was typing on her keyboard with her headset on listening in on the police scanner. It seemed to be quiet. Sara always worked Sunday evening since it was her busiest time of the week. She was responsible for the personal stuff in the paper, like obituaries and so on and on Mondays there was always more of that stuff in the paper. She looked busy.

"What?" she asked when she noticed I was looking at her.

"Could you help me out?"

She took off the headset. "Sure." She pushed the pile of letters from people wanting their stuff in the paper aside. "I'm almost done anyway."

I smiled. She was beginning to enjoy being a part of the investigating team, helping me with the research, I could tell. "I want you to find a man for me. It doesn't have to be right now, though. It can wait till the morning if you're busy with your other stuff."

"What kind of man?"

I wrote a name on a yellow note and handed it to her. She read it. "Mogens Holst?"

"He is a medical historian. He wrote a book two years ago stating that there had been cases of use of lobotomy in this country up until 1993. He later withdrew the book and his statements in it. Since then no one has heard from him. I can't find anything about him anywhere. I want to find him and talk to him. Let him know that I am on his side, when you get in contact with him."

"You seem pretty sure that I can find him?" she asked.

"I know you will," I said and sat behind my desk again. I glanced at Sara who didn't seem the least bit discouraged by her task. I was lucky to have her, I thought. She had to be the best researcher I had encountered even when I worked for the big national newspapers where they had loads of researchers working for them. None of them could do what Sara could. She could find anybody.

I grabbed the phone and called Astrupgaard Inn. I knew from the police report that the body of Susanne Larsen had been found by someone cleaning the room. All I needed now was to know who did their cleaning.

"I'm sorry. But we cannot give that kind of information out to journalists," the man answering said unfortunately. "I made the mistake of doing it once and I'm not going to do that again. It almost cost me my job."

"Let me guess, the *Express*?" I said and threw my pen on the desk.

"How did you know?" the man asked.

"Occupational hazard I guess."

I hung up. I leaned back in my chair with my arms behind my neck. It felt sore. I hadn't slept well the night before. Julie had climbed into my bed crying because she missed Tobias terribly and now she had dreamt that he was killed by that stupid killer that everybody was talking about in the news.

"Don't watch the news anymore," I had whispered. Then I had hugged her until she fell asleep. The rest of the night we had shared a pillow with the end result of a severe pain in my neck that just wouldn't go away.

I lifted my head and realized that Sune was staring at me. His eyes dropped when I looked up. I had to find a way to get him to stop longing for me somehow. It was destroying us both. I had to make it final somehow that we were never going to be together no matter what happened. There was only one way that could happen. I had to find another man.

"This Brian-guy seems to be pretty boring and pretty ordinary," Sune said. "He likes to play computer games, and it seems that the bloodier the better, but that's about all I could find. No girlfriends or secret lovers on the chat. He did watch a lot of porn, though, but that's hardly illegal."

"Some of it is. But why would he protect his computer like this if he didn't have anything to hide? Why would he run from the police?" I said. "I think he is hiding something. So keep looking."

"Okay. You're the boss."

I burst into laughter while I went for coffee in the kitchen. I brought back coffee and cake for everybody. Sara had brought a homemade cinnamon stick which was among my favorites and even if I already had a piece earlier that evening I just had to have one more. Since I hated eating alone I brought cake for everybody.

Sune smiled when I placed his in front of him. Cinnamon was among his favorites too. But that wasn't why he was smiling. "I think I might have something," he said.

"Yes?" I walked behind him and looked at the screen. A series of pictures was in front of me. "What am I looking at?"

"Ultimate violence," Sune said. "These are all thumbnails from videos that the boring Brian Poulsen has made. This is what he tried to hide from the police. This is why he's run away. He knew that when the police found these videos they would arrest him. And they will. They'll suspect him for murdering Anders Hoejmark and they'll nail him for making these and selling them on the Internet to the entire world."

"But what are they?"

"Videos of him beating up homeless people too drunk or too weak to defend themselves. Look," he said and started a video.

The camera was swinging from side to side, shaking, there were muffled voices, feet were kicking, hitting some poor defenseless man, a baseball bat was swinging and a deep moaning from someone too weak to speak filled the room.

I felt disgusted. "I don't want to watch that," I said. "Please shut it off."

Sune stopped it. Then he found some documents. "Look he even wrote stories about it. He details how they screamed for help. Quite a creative boy. He published them on the Internet on his web-page and people downloaded them for ninety-nine cents. He made quite a lot of money from it."

"That's disgusting," I said. "Do you think he killed Susanne Larsen and Anders Hoejmark?"

"I don't know," Sune said. "But he is one sick bastard that's for sure."

I exhaled and went back toward my own desk. Maybe it was about time to go home to my family; I thought when I suddenly noticed that Sara was frozen. She was wearing her headset, her body completely stiff and her eyes stared into thin air with an empty look in them. I swallowed hard. I knew exactly what that meant. I turned and looked at Sune. He had seen it too. His eyes wore the same frightened look as mine.

"Let's get ready," he said and grabbed his camera. "I'll start the car while you get the details."

## Chapter 23

THEY WERE STILL PUTTING UP CRIME TAPE WHEN WE ARRIVED AT THE scene. Three police cars were parked in front of the building. I looked for the blue van from the Forensic department but couldn't see it anywhere. We were early. An officer was talking to a young boy in a baseball cap, clearly taking his statement for the report. The boy was crying and kept covering his face with his hands.

Sune started taking pictures of the scene. I spotted Johannes Lindstroem inside the townhouse. It was pitch dark outside and the light from all the police cars were reflected in the windows of the neighbors. A small crowd of curious people was gathered not far from me. Most of them were elderly people, some walked with great difficulty with a walker others sat in wheelchairs. They were shaking their heads, whispering. They were clearly shocked and scared. This was a quiet neighborhood; this was a place where the residents normally felt safe. This was a place for those who were old but could still take care of most things themselves, and only needed someone to help every once in a while. This was better than a nursing home because the residents still had their own house, but it was a protected environment. They weren't alone. This was a safe place to be. Until now.

Sune's flash lit up the night every now and then. I walked toward the crowd to take some statements when I realized that there was more than one camera flash in the night. I turned and spotted Christian Lonstedt. He too was busy getting the best shot for the front page. I had never worked both as the journalist and photographer but wondered how he got both done. I sure didn't hope that was the future for journalists. I liked being a team, I liked working with someone, I liked having someone to talk to about the story, someone who

## Three, Four ... Better lock your door

could also contribute with his take on it, and I liked having a companion. I liked Sune.

Johannes Lindstroem exited the front door of the house. I looked at Christian. He didn't seem to see the police officer, so I hurried up and ran toward him.

"Officer Lindstroem," I said.

He turned and looked at me. "You again," he said. He smiled gently.

"What are we looking at here? Who's the victim?"

"Her name is Linda Nielsen. She was forty-six. Leaves no family behind," he said.

"Forty-six? But I thought these townhouses were supposed to be for elderly people?"

"Mostly they are. But also handicapped and people severely disabled."

"Was she handicapped or disabled?"

Johannes Lindstroem sighed deeply. "In a way she was, yes."

"How so?"

"She was big. Too big to be able to take care of herself. So the city put her here," he said. "The poor woman could hardly move on her own."

"She was so big it disabled her?" I swallowed hard. That sounded like such a waste of life.

"Yes."

"So how was she killed?" I asked. I looked into the brown eyes of Johannes Lindstroem. He didn't have to answer.

"The same," he groaned.

"Was it in the shower like the others?"

"Bathtub, but yes. Circumstances were the same. Exactly the same."

I swallowed again. He didn't have to go into details. She had been lobotomized just like the two others. Like Susanne Larsen and Anders Hoejmark.

Johannes Lindstroem's eyes seemed pensive. "I don't think I've ever encountered anything this cruel in my professional career in the force," he said. His voice was thick. This case was getting to him. It scared me to see him like that. He was the only one who could never lose it. He had to stay stable for the rest of us. If he lost it panic would surely erupt. I stared at him, waiting for him to get it together again. It was creeping me out. This whole case was.

"Do you have any leads at all?" I asked.

Johannes Lindstroem shook his head.

"What about Brian Poulsen? Have you found him yet?"

"No. We would love to start a search for him in the entire country but so far he is just a suspect. We haven't found anything linking him to the rest of the killings. Just the second one, Anders Hoejmark. He has no connection to the other victims. We have no reason for arresting him or issuing a warrant for his arrest."

"I might have some information that you ought to know," I said.

"Like what?"

I inhaled deeply. I had to be very careful now to not sell out Sune by telling what we found on the computer. "I know from a source that Brian Poulsen sells videos on the Internet of him beating homeless people half to death."

Johannes Lindstroem looked at me with disbelief. "How do you know that?"

"I can't tell. But maybe if you searched his computer really well you just might find a reason to issue that warrant."

Johannes Lindstroem nodded. "We've been trying to but not had much luck."

"I might be able to send you a file, but you have to promise me to not ask where I got it from."

Johannes Lindstroem paused. He looked at me suspiciously. Then he nodded. "Very well then. Just send it to me and I will get my best people on it right away. We'll have the entire Danish police force search for him as soon as we have the evidence." He shook my hand eagerly. "Thank you so much. It's very rare that the journalists actually help the police. Usually it's the other way around."

"Well I'm glad I could help."

Johannes Lindstroem waved at me as he walked toward his colleagues. I had given him a little help yes, but the hard part for them was still to get access to Brian Poulsen's computer. Even Sune had spent days trying. I couldn't help him with that.

"So did you get what you needed?" Christian Lonstedt had sneaked up on me from behind. I jumped at the sound of his voice.

"You startled me," I said.

He smiled gently. "Sorry. I didn't mean to."

"How long have you been there? Were you listening in on our conversation?" I asked.

"No. I already talked to Officer Lindstroem earlier." He lifted his notepad in the air. "Got all the details I needed. Scary stuff, huh?"

I scoffed. "It sure is."

I stared at Sune who was eagerly dancing around shooting pictures of everything and anyone who moved. The blue van arrived and people in blue bodysuits entered under the crime tape. Sune shot a series of pictures of them in action.

"He is good," Christian said.

"The very best," I said with a smile.

"So what's the story of you two, if you don't mind me asking?" Christian dropped his eyes when he spoke. It was kind of cute.

## Three, Four ... Better lock your door

Shyness looked good on him and made him far more attractive. I smiled.

"There is no deal. We're colleagues, that's all."

"So you've never ...?" Christian lifted his face and our eyes met. I couldn't believe he would stand here at a scene of crime and ask me a question like this. It was so inappropriate and yet a little sweet too.

"I don't think it's any of your business," I said.

He blushed and dropped his eyes again. "No of course it isn't. No I'm sorry ... I didn't mean to ... I think I'll be going now," he said and started walking.

Sune approached me with a huge smile. "I think I got some really great shots," he said. Then he showed me on the display of the camera. "Satisfied?" He asked.

I nodded. "Very. Looks like another front page."

"So what did Christian want?" Sune asked.

"What? Oh nothing. Just chatting."

"He has become quite chatty lately," Sune said.

"Well he is new to the area. Maybe he's just looking for friends."

"Maybe," Sune said. "So now what, boss?"

I interviewed the pizza delivery boy and then the scared elderly people living in the area they used to consider so safe and Sune took some pictures of them for the second article. They were all very good. The pizza delivery boy told in detail how he had entered the house with the pizza and then saw the flood of blood on the ground. He cried when I asked what the body looked like, so I didn't ask him for more specifics about it. The blood on the floor was scary enough. Jens-Ole had to make do with that.

Sune and I both waited till the body left the house and was taken away in an ambulance before we drove back to the office in silence. I wrote two articles that made it to my editor just in time for deadline.

## Chapter 24

I SLEPT IN THE NEXT DAY. OR AT LEAST I TRIED TO. I THOUGHT I HAD deserved it after the long day I had the day before. My article about the history of lobotomy had been postponed since the new killing filled most of the paper so my editor told me to take it easy and come in before lunch. He already had an article for the next day's paper, so I didn't have to write anything new.

Dad made sure Julie got in school on time while I took an extra hour in bed. It felt good to rest a little even if I did have a hard time relaxing. I wondered about all the killings. I kept seeing the pictures of Susanne Larsen from the police report. This was the killer's third victim, so now we could definitely call him a serial killer. He did seem to have his rituals and used the same modus operandi on all of his victims. But where was the connection? Were they all random victims? Did he get his satisfaction from the ritual of the kill? Or was there something deeper to this?

I realized I wasn't going to get any more sleep so I got out of bed and got dressed. I ran downstairs and grabbed a piece of toast that Dad had left out for me.

Five minutes later I entered the editorial room with my laptop under my arm. Sara looked at me.

"I thought you were going to sleep in today?"

"Me too," I said with a smile. I sat at my desk and opened my computer. Julie was smiling at me from my screen. I hadn't spent much time with her lately, I thought. I had to make it up to her somehow. I didn't want to abandon her like her father had. She needed me more than ever since I was the only parent in her life right now.

"Found your guy for you," Sara said and waved a yellow post-it note in the air.

## Three, Four ... Better lock your door

"My guy? Mogens Holst?" I asked.

"Yup. Wasn't easy though. But once I saw his picture on the Internet I knew I had seen him somewhere. Turns out I had. He lives in the basement of the house next to one of my sister's friends. Doesn't look like the picture much anymore, though. He's grown a beard and lost a lot of weight. But it's definitely him. I checked with the National Registry and there is a Mogens Lundgreen living on that address. I found out that Lundgreen was his mother's maiden name."

I looked at her impressed. Sara knew everybody around here. "Does that mean he's in our area?"

"Sure does. He lives just outside of Naestved at old Olsen's farm. It was closed down a couple of years ago when the owner Bjarke Olsen died. The wife, Esther, lives there alone and rents out the basement. She sold off all the land and lives off the money now. "

"That is great news. But changing his last name also means that he doesn't want to be found. So I'd better not call in advance."

"You're certain that you want to talk to this guy?" Sara asked.

"Very. Why?"

"Everything I've found about him states that he's a fraud. His book, his research. Everything is phony."

I exhaled knowing that she might be right.

Sune entered the door whistling a Frank Sinatra song.

"I thought he wasn't working today?" Sara looked at me. "You're not doing an article for tomorrow, are you?"

"No, but I called him in anyway," I said and waved at him. "I need his help for something else and yours too."

"I want you to go through all three police-reports and the Internet and find out every detail you can about the victims," I said to Sara and Sune as soon as he had taken off his jacket and gotten his first cup of coffee from the kitchen.

Sune nodded, sipping his coffee. Sara listened with a focused look.

"I want to know where they are from, where they went to school, if they have any siblings, children or other family members, where they worked, marriage status, basically everything about them. I want to know if there is any connection between them - anything at all. Even small things like they all ate the same type of chocolate or drank the same drink in the same bar or something like that. Whatever you can find that could link these three people together. I know the police are probably doing the exact same thing right now, but if there is a connection I want to be first with the story. I really want to be the one to stop people from being afraid. As the situation is right now everybody is a possible victim and that creates fear among people. I know I'm afraid for my family and you have probably thought about it too."

Both Sune and Sara nodded. I continued:

"I for one want to find some kind of pattern here so I don't have to fear one of my loved ones will be the next victim. Can you help me do that?"

Sara and Sune looked at each other and nodded. "Sure," they said in unison.

"Great. Meanwhile I'll pay Mogens Lundgreen a visit."

It was raining when I drove towards Naestved. The farm was situated somewhere in the middle between Karrebaeksminde and Naestved. As soon as I was out of town the hilly landscape revealed all its beauty. The dark clouds heavy with rain gave it an obscure light. It was a little gloomy. Fall in Denmark always made me feel melancholy, I thought as I drove through the bare hills and vast and empty landscape. The leaves on the trees were in so many colors now. It was beautiful, splendid, an explosion of colors. It was only for a few weeks every year that you got to enjoy the many orange and brown colors on the trees. Soon they would all be on the ground and soon after that they would be gone. The trees would be barren for months and months while darkness ruled all winter. Like Julie would say when she was younger, the trees looked like they were "broken." The temperature had already dropped a lot the last few days and I turned on the heat in the car. Now I opened the window for a few minutes just to feel the air. That was the one thing I did like at this time of year. It was so crisp and clear. But soon it would be so cold it would be biting in my cheeks.

I sighed and closed the window again. I loved summer and this year we had had more of it than we could ever hope for, but it always filled me with great sadness to see it go, it was like saying goodbye to an old friend every time. One you knew you'd miss insanely in just a few weeks.

The old farm house looked sinister in the darkness from the sky above. I drove up the long driveway and parked the car in the gravel in front of it. It had stopped raining but a cold North wind hit me in the face and reminded me again that winter was right around the corner. In a little over a month the darkness would take over. I shivered at the thought.

It was an old and worn building. Walls were cracking and paint peeling. The grass had grown wild and weeds were growing between tiles and cracks in the stairs leading to the main entrance. Stairs lead down to the basement. I walked down. The door had a frosted window. I knocked.

A dog started barking but there was no answer. I knocked again.

# Three, Four ... Better lock your door

"Hello?" I yelled. "Is anyone here?"

Still no answer. It started to rain again. The cold wind made it feel like ice hitting my face. Damn weather. No wonder people were depressed in this country. From now on and until Christmas it would only get worse. The days would get shorter and darker. The sun would rise late - around eight - and set around four in the afternoon. Some days we wouldn't even see the sun because of the heavy gray clouds. Anyone who was outdoors would hurry to get back inside; people would rush to work, to their cars, to the shed at the bus stop to get shelter. People would walk huddled, crouching to avoid getting the cold wind and rain in their face. The lack of sun made us tired, irritable and we hardly had the energy to look at each other or even say hello to anyone we didn't know.

I sighed and knocked again.

The dog was barking wildly behind the door. Then there was another sound on the other side of the door. A rattle, like someone was putting on a chain to keep the door from being able to open entirely. I inhaled. This would require usage of my best and most developed skills of persuasion.

The door squeaked and opened slightly. A set of eyes appeared under the chain. Underneath them a pit-bull showed its face. It was white with red eyes. I stepped backwards. The dog was held back. It snarled and barked. Someone hushed it and told it to go back.

"Mr. Lundgreen?" I said.

"What do you want?" The voice was hoarse and hostile.

"I'm Rebekka Franck. I work for *Zeeland Times*."

"I know who you are," he said. "I asked you what you wanted not who you were."

"Okay. I am here to talk to you. Off the record if you prefer. I just need to know a little about your book. I want to know about the lobotomies."

There was a long silence. It felt really uncomfortable.

"Are you alone?" He asked.

"Yes."

"No photographer?"

"No. So far it's only research."

"What's your angle?"

"I don't know yet. I was hoping you could tell me," I said.

The eyes stared at me in disbelief. Then he closed the door. For a second I thought I had lost him, but I heard a rattle once again and now the door was opened entirely.

"Come on in."

## Chapter 25

THE SMALL ROOM IN THE BASEMENT WAS A DUMP. IT WAS DARK AND dim. Only two dirty small windows under the ceiling brought in the daylight. It smelled terrible. Dirty glasses and plates with days of leftovers stuck to it in the sink. Old empty beer bottles on the coffee table told me that Mogens Holst probably wasn't sober. His hands were shaking as he removed some newspapers from a brown chair and told me to sit. A plant in a pot on the table had died a long time ago and had crumbled up and turned black and white.

Mogens Holst took a cigarette from a package and lit it. I considered asking if I could have one but resisted the temptation. I had quit and didn't want to start again now. Mogens Holst inhaled desperately on the cigarette. His hands were shaking as he moved it to the full ashtray in the middle of the table.

"You're sure no one knows you came here?" he asked. His voice trembled slightly. He looked at the front door nervously, then at the window behind him. I couldn't quite figure him out, if he was a lunatic. The pit-bull sat in the corner growling and staring at me.

"Pretty sure. Why?"

"No reason." He shook his head. "So what do you want to know?"

"You wrote a book about the usage of lobotomies here in Denmark stating that you had documentation that said it was used all the way into the Nineties. What kind of documentation did you have?"

Mogens Holst sniffed and killed his cigarette in the ashtray.

"Could I see it?" I asked.

He looked at me with skepticism. It made me feel uncomfortable. Maybe Irene Hoeg had been right. Maybe he was a nutcase. But if he had the documentation then I wanted to see it. I felt there was a story there for me to tell.

"Why? What do you want to do with it?" he asked. "You know I have withdrawn the book, right? You do realize that I had to take it all back afterwards? No one believes in a word I said back then."

I know. That's something I wanted to talk to you about as well. Why did you withdraw everything?"

Mogens Holst sighed. "I had to. The bastards forced me."

"Who did?"

He exhaled deeply. He picked up the pack of cigarettes and took out another one. The room was getting heavy with smoke as he lit the next one.

"They ruined my name," he said. "Cost me everything. My work, my family."

"Who? How?" I asked.

"I never found out exactly who was behind it. I do however have a pretty good picture of who it might have been. It happened over a short period of time. It started with my research funding being stopped suddenly. Then the university threw me out. Said my research wasn't valuable, told me I had been falsifying results. Later my publisher withdrew the book and told me to go public and apologize. Tell the world that I was wrong. Then my story was all over the media, the story about me being a drunk, a schizophrenic who was now self-medicating with alcohol. No one wanted to hear what I said anymore. Lost all my credibility, they said. The truth was drowned in a smear campaign about my personality."

"Why would they say all those things?" I asked.

He looked at me. Then he burst into laughter that led to a hoarse cough. "Because I am. They found my papers that stated I had been admitted several times to a mental institution when I was younger."

"So it wasn't a lie?"

Mogens Holst leaned over the table. He stared at me with narrow eyes. "No it's true alright. But I never falsified those documents. Anyone who sees them will know they're true. I knew when I found them that this was explosive material. I just didn't realize how far into the system it reached."

"How far did it reach?"

"This is so big. It can overthrow the government. I didn't know it when I wrote the book, it wasn't until later that I realized that the current prime minister knows that these things have taken place and she has chosen to hide it. She was the minister of the department of health from 1990-1994. She was the one who approved it. Our current prime-minister, the leader of this country is responsible for this happening. If this is revealed she will be forced to resign."

I gasped. My heart was racing in my chest. This was an even

bigger story than I had expected. "What did they approve? The usage of lobotomy?"

"They lobotomized kids all the way into the nineties. The last I have found record of was conducted in 1993."

"Wow. But they say that the use of lobotomy ended in the late Seventies?" I said.

"That's the story they are sticking to, yes. But it didn't. There was a place here close to Karrebaeksminde - Lundegaarden - where they sent criminal children and teenagers that they had no idea what to do with. They used them as lab rats, as experiments. The doctors there had a theory. They believed that the criminals were born with a defect in the brain that they could somehow fix. That was why they deviated, that was why they displayed such cruelty and indifference to other people. You have to remember that these kids were bad news; they were killers and rapists at a very young age. They were somebody no one wanted in society, someone they would have placed on a deserted island if possible. But they were too young to go to prison. So the doctors had a theory that they could somehow fix what was wrong with them. They just needed to find the right "wires" to cut, so to speak. They thought they could somehow "cut the evil out of them." That was how it was presented to the minister of health back then. They were certain they had detected where the defect was in the brain that caused these kids to be evil. They thought they had found a way they could help these young people to get a normal life, a way to cure them so to speak."

"By lobotomizing them?" I asked startled.

Mogens Holst nodded. "They said that they had found a new method. That back in the days when they had done it on psychiatric patients they cut the wrong nerve paths. That was why it went wrong. But these doctors were certain they could do this right and make Denmark known all over the world for this research. Imagine being able to cure criminal teenagers? Imagine how much money the government would save on juvenile prisons and personnel by removing this burden, by pacifying these criminals who didn't contribute anything to our society and make them no longer a threat to ordinary decent people?"

"But what happened to them?" I asked still shocked at how this could have happened less than twenty years ago.

"They became apathetic of course. Some even died from brain damage. But it wasn't spoken about. No one ever missed them. In the system they weren't considered human. They were experiments. Their lives had no value."

I stared at Mogens Holst in shock. I couldn't believe him. I didn't want to believe him. I shook my head.

## Three, Four ... Better lock your door

"This is horrible," I said. "You have the documentation for all this?"

He nodded with a smile. "I do."

"Could I see it?"

Mogens Holst got up from the couch. He went into another room and then returned shortly after. A huge stack of files and papers landed on the desk in front of me. "You can have it all. Never did me any good. No one will ever believe me again. Not after they destroyed my name. My own wife even turned her back at me. Didn't believe I was right in my mind any longer, she said." Mogens Holst scoffed. "Maybe she was right. Look at me now. I'm a drunk and a lowlife. Nobody cares anymore."

I stared at the piles of paper. I had no idea what to do with this material, with this story. Would the paper run it? Would they dare?

Mogens Holst had put a copy of his book on top of the pile. I took it and read the back. According to the text there had been "many operations performed on children as young as eight years of age, even though their brains were not yet completely developed."

I leaned back in my chair shocked by this. I couldn't believe that they had actually done this to children. I thought about what we did to them today. Drugging them with all kinds of things if they turned out to be just a little wild or uncontrollable. It seemed that the medical world had always been trying to explain deviant behavior and responding to it with medicine or surgery. These were children we were talking about. Criminals or not. This was not right. It had to be told.

I got up from the chair and grabbed all the files and papers.

"I hope you'll have more luck with this than I had," said Mogens Holst as I walked toward the door. He held it open for me.

I sighed. "I really hope I will too," I said.

## Chapter 26

I BROKE OUT IN A COLD SWEAT WHILE I DROVE BACK TOWARDS Karrebaeksminde. The papers and files were in the back seat. This was huge, I thought. This could be the story of my career. This kind of stuff could make or break a career. It was every journalist's dream to come across material like this that could overthrow a government.

It had to have been the same for Mogens Holst as well back when he discovered this. It must have been the highlight of his career for him, the research, the book everything had to have been so big, and then ... then he was destroyed. Was that going to happen to me too if I chose to write the story? But what could they do to me? Disgrace my name? Discredit my career? Could I do this and not care about my future, about the price I would have to pay?

I wasn't sure. Yet I wasn't sure I could afford not to write this.

I parked the car in my usual parking spot and walked towards the office building. The streets were empty. Deserted, vacant, abandoned. Most of the small shops in the main street were closed down. Only a few remained open even if they knew nobody was going to come. Fear was slowly killing the town. People gave into their fear and stayed home. They only went out when it was absolutely necessary. Like going to work or going to school in the morning. Nobody went out for fun or at night, nobody shopped except for groceries, nobody went out to eat at the restaurants or stayed at the hotels. This was really bad. Everybody kept inside their houses, curtains closed, waiting for the next murder to happen, fearing they would be the next victim. How long was this supposed to go on? How long could the town survive this?

I opened the door and went up the stairs carrying the files and papers in my arms. With great difficulty I managed to open the door

## Three, Four ... Better lock your door

to the editorial room by pushing it with my back. Sune came to my rescue.

"Here let me grab some of that," he said and took the papers out of my hands. "What is all this?"

I exhaled and took off my jacket. "I'm not sure," I said. "It might just be the biggest story of my career or it might be the end of it."

I smiled. Then I told him what Mogens Holst had said and what I expected to find in the secret files. Sune and Sara were both shocked.

"So how are you doing here?" I looked at Sara and then at Sune. They had put up a whiteboard in the room and written all over it. I approached it.

"We tried to paint a picture of the three victims by writing down anything we found about them that could have any interest," Sune said and pointed at Susanne Larsen's name that was written on top. "For example we know Susanne Larsen was a mother of two, a boy and a girl, and she was married to a police officer in Naestved. We also know that she worked as a nurse at Naestved Hospital ..."

"What kind of nurse was she?" I asked.

Sune shook his head. "I don't know."

"I need that information too. I need everything. Everything looks great though. Very thorough."

"She was in palliative care," Sara said. "She helped patients who suffered from brain tumors or mental dysfunctions."

"Great. Put it down for me will you?"

Sara wrote it under Susanne Larsen's name. I stared at the whiteboard, studied it. I read where they went to school, where they grew up, about Susanne Larsen's husband and their children, about Anders Hoejmark's love for badminton that later lead to his job as the president of the club, about Linda Nielsen's severe depression that had started as many as twenty years ago and caused her to start overeating and be declared unable to work. I tried all I could but I didn't see any connection. Not an obvious one at least.

I grabbed a chair and stared at the whiteboard for a long time. Sune brought me a cup of coffee that I drank while thinking. All the information the last couple of days was mixed in my head, all the theories, all the thoughts, everything there had been said was twirling around in my head until I had a thought, an idea.

"What if ...?" I said.

Sune and Sara looked closely at me with anticipating eyes like they had expected me to speak a long time ago.

"Let's say that someone knew about this work that they did at Lundegaarden with the criminal children or maybe that person was even a part of it and believed that they could in fact help people with deviant behavior. Help them become normal or at least somewhat pacified and relieved from whatever made them do what they had done, relieved from being evil."

Sune and Sara stared at me with great skepticism.

"Just follow me here," I said. "Keep an open mind. Let's say that this person - who by the way must be out of his mind - but this person wants to keep doing these lobotomies and continue the work they began, maybe even thinking they were working for a good cause. Maybe he lost it recently and suddenly got the idea that he could help or maybe even get rid of people who were somehow wrong or who didn't behave right."

Sune looked like he understood. "You think the killer used to work at Lundegaarden and used to perform these lobotomies?"

I nodded. "It's a wild theory, I know."

"But Susanne Larsen, Anders Hoejmark nor Linda Nielsen were criminals."

"Maybe the killer is not getting rid of criminals but just people displaying morally wrong behavior, morally decadent. You see where I am going?"

Sara sighed. "But how do the victims fit into that?"

"Linda Nielsen was kind of disabled. She was declared unfit to work and could hardly take care of herself. But there wasn't anything really wrong with her physically that she hadn't afflicted upon herself through her depression. So maybe the killer sees it as morally bad behavior. She is a problem for society, she costs money, and she doesn't contribute."

"Just like the young criminals," Sune said.

"Exactly," I continued. "According to Mogens Holst that was the way they saw the children at Lundegaarden, as a burden. Their illness was something that had to be cured. Maybe this person is trying to 'clean up' if you know what I mean."

"But what about the other two?" Sune asked.

"Susanne Larsen was unfaithful to her husband and not just having an affair like most do in cases of infidelity. She was having S&M - sex with strangers at hotels while her husband knew nothing of it."

"That's bad moral behavior alright," Sune said. "And Anders Hoejmark?"

I shrugged. "Well he was gay. It said so in the police report. People in the club told the police that they all knew he was gay but he was trying to hide it. They also said that there were rumors about him having sex with men in the men's dressing room after closing time, but they were never confirmed."

Sune and Sara looked at me while nodding. "Sounds like we have a plausible theory," Sune said.

"So the killer is someone who used to work at Lundegaarden?" Sara repeated.

"He could be," I answered, "but again he could be someone just inspired by what they did."

"Like Mogens Holst," Sune exclaimed.

I looked at him with surprise. I hadn't thought about that angle. "I don't know about that," I said. "He doesn't seem to be the type. He has more of a sad existence."

"But he knows more about this than anyone else. Plus he is mad at the world for being wronged," Sune argued.

"Plus he is a schizophrenic," I mumbled. "And a drunk." I stared at the whiteboard while all these thoughts ran through my head. There was something here, we were definitely on to something, but I just couldn't quite figure out all the details.

"What do you think, Rebekka?" Sara asked.

"I was thinking about Irene Hoeg," I said.

"The doctor you interviewed about lobotomy. Why are you thinking about her?" Sara asked.

"It was something she said. Like she approved of the use of lobotomy. She said she had done it on one patient back in the seventies and even though the patient ended up like an apathetic vegetable then it was a better life for her than what she had. At least she was relieved of her pain and struggle inside of her."

"I think that you could find several doctors still advocating for these kinds of methods," Sune said. "Sad as it is."

I smiled. "I think so too. Maybe we should try and find out. Our killer might be one of them."

## Chapter 27

We found a handful of people, especially doctors who were known to have advocated the use of lobotomy in the media over the last fifty years. Three of them were already dead and that only left us with two. Irene Hoeg was one of them and also the most prominent, a doctor Arthur Sejr Andersen was the other. But he was eighty-three and lived in a nursing home.

I stared at the list a little resignedly. Sune stood beside me.

"Could it be Irene Hoeg?" he asked. "Could she be the killer?"

"Except that we are looking for a man," I said.

"Why?"

"Because they found semen in Susanne Larsen and Anders Hoejmark was a big guy. The police said he was held down by the throat while the lobotomy was completed," I said.

Sune nodded and sipped his coffee. "Sure but couldn't the semen belong to the lover that Susanne Larsen was with, the one she met up with, and who maybe just fled the scene to not have his identity revealed? Couldn't a very strong woman be able to hold down Anders Hoejmark?"

"Irene Hoeg is a fairly strong and tall woman. Her handshake hurt my hand," I said pensively. "So you're thinking that Susanne Larsen actually met with some other man, someone who was not the killer and then the killer showed up?"

"Yes. Let's imagine the man she is with is married and has a great job and career. He doesn't want to risk losing anything by coming forward and telling the police what he knows."

"And Brian Poulsen?" I asked and pointed at his name that was written on the whiteboard under suspects.

"Same thing. Knew he was in trouble if they found his videos on the computer and took off."

"But why would Irene Hoeg travel all the way to Karrebaeksminde to commit these killings? Why not do it closer to where she lives?" Sara asked.

"Because that would be too obvious. Too dangerous. The woman is smart and not planning on being caught," I said.

"But why Karrebaeksminde of all places?" Sara asked.

I shrugged. "I don't know." I looked at Sune.

He smiled. "I know what you're thinking," he said. "We need to check the forensic reports again." Sune walked fast towards his computer. "We haven't even looked at Linda Nielsen's yet. Maybe there is something."

"You took the words right out of my mouth. That was precisely what I was thinking," I said. I grabbed a chair and pulled it up next to Sune's.

His fingers danced across the keyboard. Soon he was in the police's database and opened the report on Linda Nielsen's death. The pictures were brutal and we hurried past them assuming they were much like the previous two. Sune scrolled and read the text rapidly. His lips moved as he read.

"There," he said and pointed at the screen.

I looked and felt my heart racing in my chest. They had found blond hair near Linda's body. Long blond hair that they assumed belonged to a woman.

It was all just a very loose theory so far but it kind of stuck with me, with all of us at the paper for the rest of the day. We had no evidence, we had nothing but thoughts and ideas so we couldn't talk to the police about it yet, but still we couldn't stop thinking about it. I looked at the huge pile of papers I had received from Mogens Holst. I wanted to start reading them, I wanted to be prepared so I could talk to Jens-Ole about running the story, but I couldn't focus, I couldn't concentrate. If it turned out to be Irene Hoeg who was killing these people then who could stop her? Were the police even on to her? Had they investigated her?

Evidence or not I grabbed the phone and called the head of Karrebaeksminde police department.

"I know this will sound weird but have you investigated Dr. Irene Hoeg? She is one of the few doctors in the country who has actually performed a lobotomy and I recently did an interview with her where she clearly stated that she thought it had actually helped people back in the days when they used it. I don't know if there is anything to it, but I just thought ..."

Johannes Lindstroem interrupted me. "Let me just stop you right there," he said. "We have already spoken to the doctor and she has a clear alibi for all three nights when the victims were killed."

"Oh. Okay," I stuttered quite startled.

"Was there anything else?"

"Well I wanted to ask you if it is true that you are considering the possibility that the killer might be a woman, but I think you kind of already answered that."

"I guess I just did. Good day then."

"Good day."

I hung up and looked at Sune. "At least we can now run the story that the police think the killer might be a woman," I said.

I called up Jens-Ole and he was ecstatic. "Write, God damn it. Write the article. We're running it in the morning. 'Lobotomy-killer could be a woman,' I love it. This just gets better and better."

He hung up. I wrote the story and sent it. Afterwards I wrote a shorter version and sent it to the guys doing our on-line newspaper. I looked up the *Express*' online paper and found nothing like it. We were first again, I thought with satisfaction. First, before Christian Lonstedt and his perfect smile.

Then I went home to Dad and Julie.

I had barely gotten inside of the house and hugged my daughter when the phone rang. Julie gave me one of those "You're a terrible mother" looks.

"Sorry sweetie, but I better answer this. It might be important." I looked at the display. Private number it said. I answered it.

"Rebekka Franck."

"Christian Lonstedt."

I froze while looking for something clever and bright to say. I was kind of caught off guard here. I felt so foolish, but I actually blushed. I was beginning to wonder if I actually liked this guy. I had no idea why I would. He was insanely annoying, everything about him irritated me, but I was beginning to think that maybe, just maybe he was the type that grew on you. Ever since that evening he had stopped by the paper I realized that there might be more to him than what I first anticipated. His experience in Africa had left an impact on me. I was beginning to suspect that I hadn't given him enough credit in the beginning. I hated to admit it, but I was open for a reevaluation.

"Christian. What can I do for you?" I asked expecting his call to be merely professional. As usual I put up all my guards suspecting that he wanted something from me, that he wanted to pump me for information.

"First of all, congrats on your story tonight about the killer being female. I just read it online. Everybody will be quoting you for this in the morning," he said.

I felt a wrinkle form in my forehead. What was this? Was he complimenting me? Was this some sort of trick? What did he want? He had to have an ulterior motive. There just had to be. "Well thanks. I was lucky, I guess. You know how it is sometimes," I said. My dad's cat was staring at me from the windowsill. Even she could hear how stupid I sounded.

"I'm never that lucky," he said gently. "You're really good."

"Um ... thanks?" I said not knowing how to deal with this, how to react. What was this? What did he want? "And second of all?" I asked.

"Oh yeah. Second of all I wanted to apologize for my bad behavior the other day. It wasn't tactful. It was insensitive and rude to ask you that question."

I laughed lightly. "You don't have to apologize. I'm not that easy to offend," I said.

"Well, I'd like to make it up to you by inviting you for dinner. I don't know anyone in this area and I could really use a night out. Does Wednesday night sound okay?"

I hesitated. I didn't know what to say. I guess he took me off guard once again. I wasn't prepared for this. Plus I didn't understand what he wanted. Was it a date-date? Or just a friend-date because he was lonely in a new area?

"Your pause makes me quite uncomfortable," he continued. He sounded so correct and polite. It was sweet.

"I'm so sorry. I didn't mean to imply that I was reluctant. I'm just a little surprised that's all. Plus we are competitors in a way so I guess I was wondering if there could be an ulterior motive. But of course there isn't. You're not that type. I know. Forgive me. I'm just paranoid, I guess."

"You're rambling," he said.

I laughed. "Yes. I'm sorry. I ... I'm just ..."

"Just a simple yes or no would soothe my unease," he said.

I exhaled.

"Then it is a yes."

## Chapter 28

MARTIN FRANDSEN WAS A QUIET MAN. HE ENJOYED THE CALM DAYS OF his early retirement. He liked to read the paper, go for a long walk on the beach or in the forest. He enjoyed a good dinner prepared for him by his wife of forty years, he loved reading a good book, preferable a mystery - while sitting in the quiet corner of the living room with nothing but a lamp lit over his head. He didn't care much for other people. They were noisy and they always wanted something from him. Especially his children and grandchildren. He liked seeing them every now and then, but they disturbed his peace, they interfered with the calmness in his mind that he worked so hard every day to obtain.

And so did his wife. Marianne Frandsen was a very noisy woman and over the years she hadn't exactly become quieter. She always wanted something from him. She wanted him to clean up the garage, fix the sink when it was clogged, and take out the trash. She always wanted something from him and Martin Frandsen found himself often trying to escape her voice by hiding from her either in the bathroom, the basement or the garage. And she always talked. Boy did she talk. The mouth never stood still on that woman. She would talk and talk about everything and nothing; about the neighbor's cat that looked weird because it had grown a lump on the side of its face, their daughter's new job and colleagues that Martin Frandsen would never meet and therefore couldn't care less about. Marianne would try and pick a fight with him just to get him to talk to her. She would nag him about his reading, his quietness and silence that she didn't understand. She would say that he had stalled, that he needed to pull himself out of this. He had even heard her talk to their grown son about him. They asked each other if it could be depression. That maybe Martin had a hard time accepting that he wasn't going to work anymore, that he wasn't needed any longer? Their son who was a doctor had told her that often elderly people became depressed.

Martin Frandsen let them talk. He didn't care much about any of them anyway. He wasn't depressed and he certainly wasn't an elderly man. He was just trying to finally enjoy life, enjoy his retirement and listen to the birds. But he could never get to hear them since there was always someone talking.

Martin Frandsen thought about leaving his wife every day. He wasn't sure he even loved her anymore; it was hard to say that he loved anything at all except for the few quiet moments he stole during the day. Today he considered leaving her more than ever.

After lunch Marianne Frandsen told her husband that she wanted them to try something new. She had the idea that all they needed was to spice up their sex-life. Then everything would be better. She thought that she could get her husband out of this depression-like state of his by giving their sex-life something new, something more exciting.

"Like the couple down the street did. The Jensens. They started going to this swinger-club. Spiced up everything in their life," she said. "The husband became a brand new person. Gitte Jensen told me that it was like getting an entirely new husband."

Martin Frandsen stared at his wife with great suspicion and wide open eyes. "Maybe you need a new husband," he answered slightly hoping that she would take him up on his word.

Marianne Frandsen tapped him on his shoulder with an "Oh you silly old man" and a laugh to match it. Then she stood up and looked at him. "I have arranged for everything," she said. "He'll be here at six."

"Who will be here at six?" Martin Frandsen asked while his wife started removing their plates from the table.

"You'll see," she said with a vicious smile.

That was when Martin Frandsen seriously considered to start packing his belongings and moving for good. But where would he go? Who would cook for him while he searched for a quiet moment?

Martin Frandsen sighed deeply and sat in his favorite chair in the corner of the living room. Then he picked up his book and started reading. If his wife wanted to spice up their sex-life then so be it. She could do whatever she wanted. He didn't care. At least she had stopped talking for a little while.

## Chapter 29

The doorbell rang at precisely six o'clock. Martin Frandsen exhaled deeply and stared into the darkness outside the windows.

"Here he is," sang Marianne as she ran towards the door. She was dressed - well she was hardly dressed at all. She was wearing long stockings that made her look like a fish caught in a net. They were too small for her so the flesh bulged out in all the holes. She had also put her body into some red satin lingerie garment with open front top that didn't cover her breasts but made them stick out and look all puffed and lumpy. The panties were tied across her front and let nothing be left to the imagination.

"Well come on," she hissed at Martin and urged him to get up now from his old brown recliner.

He sighed and put his book down. Then he did as she wanted and got up. Marianne grabbed his arm and held on to him shivering with excitement. "Remember this is for the both of us," she whispered. "Isn't it thrilling?"

"What about dinner?" he asked grumbling. "We always eat at six-thirty. You know I get a headache if I don't eat. When are we supposed to eat?"

Martin never got his answer before Marianne opened the door with a huge smile and a man's face was revealed. He was tall and extremely handsome, almost intimidating for Martin who had never been much of a looker himself.

"Come on in," Marianne said and held the door open for the man.

He moved with long and delicate movements when he walked, he was almost graceful. Martin was startled. He had never seen such a beautiful man and to his surprise he was quite intrigued.

## Three, Four ... Better lock your door

"Isn't he gorgeous?" Marianne exclaimed almost electrified when she stared at his behind in the tight jeans. "It was Linette down at the golf club that put me in contact with him. He does only couples," she said.

Martin stared at the handsome guy who seemed to be lighting up the entire living room with nothing but his mere presence. He still didn't know what this man was supposed to do but he was suddenly very curious to find out. The man smiled and winked at Martin. It caused him to blush like a school girl.

"Do you want to start down here or go directly upstairs?" the man asked, smiling.

Even his voice was God-like. Never had Martin heard such a voice that in no way irritated him, he didn't even wish it would go away. Now this was a voice he could listen to all day long. It was none of all that high-pitched shrill sounds that Martin was used to that were always complaining, nit-picking and fault-finding. No this was a bass. These were low tunes, this was manly and it was calming, almost soothing to Martin's tortured soul.

"Let's go upstairs," Marianne sang lightly. "We don't want any neighbors to watch through those big windows."

The man smiled. He was an Adonis. If there ever was a God of beauty and desire, he was it, Martin thought. The man took his bag and started up the stairs.

"Are you coming?" he said to Martin.

"He just needs a little time to come around to this," Marianne said and walked ahead of them up the stairs in her black latex extremely high-heeled shoes. "He is a slow starter, if you know what I mean. But at least it's better than a quick finisher. Am I right?" Then she laughed incredibly loudly.

The sound of her voice felt like knives on Martin's skin.

"Come on," the man said to Martin while he reached out his hand toward him. "I won't bite. Not unless you ask me to."

Martin swallowed hard before he could find the courage to accept the invitation. He thought about running away a couple of times. Just back up, go through the front door and start running. But he had been running all of his life, hadn't he? Running from the past, running from the pain, running from pleasure, running from anything that would make him feel. Escaping into the world of books, into the world of killers in his mysteries that did worse things than what he had done. Maybe now it was time. Time to start living again. Martin exhaled deeply and put his hand inside the beautiful Adonis'.

"There you go," the man said and pulled him closer. He even smelled sexy. It stirred Martin up inside.

The Adonis held Martin's hand all the way up the stairs and led him gently through the hallway. In the bedroom Marianne had made herself comfortable. She was lying on top of the bed in an inviting position. She was calling for the man to come in and join her. The Adonis looked at Martin and smiled again. He leaned towards him. His lips touched his ear when he spoke.

Martin felt a chill in his neck that caused his skin to shiver.

"I can tell that you're uncomfortable with this," the Adonis whispered. "That's only natural. Maybe if you go to the bathroom and take a shower to calm you down. I'll take good care of your wife first and then I'll come and join you. Maybe we can all do something afterwards. Okay?"

Martin smiled. It sounded like something he would enjoy. Being alone with the Adonis in the shower, as far away from Marianne's shrieking voice as possible, a voice that would always become worse during excitement and sex. The water would drown any sound coming from the bedroom. Yes that was a really good idea, Martin thought and left the two of them alone in the bedroom.

As he undressed himself in the bathroom revealing his aging body he heard Marianne giggle and laugh. Then there was moaning. He put his ear to the wall. He liked the sound of the Adonis moaning when he entered his wife. Martin imagined how big his sex had to be. Marianne screamed with joy. Oh the pleasure this was going to be. The pictures of the man on top of his wife, sweating, his muscles vibrating under the skin, a vein in the forehead popping up from the exertion, pulsating under the tanned glistening skin. He was rough on her he could hear. The sound of two bodies slapping against each other aroused Martin like nothing had ever done before. The pictures in his head of the man, the Adonis penetrating Marianne hard, riding her, exploiting her, using her body for mere pleasure. Shutting her up with his big sex.

It was exhilarating.

When they went quiet in the bedroom Martin hurried up and turned on the water. He jumped in and let the soft water caress his body. Never had he felt more alive than in this moment. He was frightened, excited, aroused at the same time. The expectation, the waiting for this man, this body that would soon be close to his made him on the verge of explosion. He had to restrain himself.

The door was opened. Martin gasped with delight. This was it. He was in the room. The Adonis was close now. Martin could almost hear his breath. In a minute he would pull the curtain to the shower and be right there behind him, naked, sweaty, the scent of his wife all over him. Martin shivered with pleasure. His sex was hard. He was ready for this, he was ready for him. Oh the wait was unbearable yet so thrilling.

Finally the curtain was pulled aside. Martin closed his eyes. He didn't dare to look at this forbidden pleasure. He was embarrassed by

## Three, Four ... Better lock your door

his lust, by his desire for another man, yet he wanted this to happen more than anything in the world.

And he really wanted to see it, to experience it, to remember it afterwards. He wanted to see him, the beautiful man that he felt so attracted to. So he opened his eyes and turned his head to look at this handsome man only to face an ugly truth from his past. One he thought he had managed to forget. A tall woman dressed in a long blue sparkling evening dress was standing right next to him with a scalpel in her hand.

She was giggling like a little girl.

## Chapter 30

MARIANNE FRANDSEN FELT JOYFUL WHEN SHE WOKE UP IN HER BED the next morning. She felt like singing. So filled with pleasure and peace. Birds were chirping outside her window. It was still early but the sun had just begun to rise. She turned over in bed and realized that he was still there. The handsome man who had swept her off her feet the night before. She smiled and laughed to herself remembering all the things they had done. Oh ... all those positions she didn't know were even possible. She had no idea that sex could be so wonderful, so filled with pleasure and desire. With Martin it had always been something that had to be done, like a duty, a wife's duty towards her husband. Martin was so clumsy, so distant, and so indifferent.

But not this guy. This man was all there. He had taken her and made her into the woman she always knew she could become. She stared at his upper arm on top of the comforter. She wanted to touch those muscles. She wanted to feel them. She remembered how they had pulsated under the skin while he was on top of her; how they had held her down while he penetrated her. And those hands, those strong hands. They had held her throat, almost suffocated her when she came, causing the orgasm to be so much stronger, overwhelming and powerful. Then he had let go and she had gasped for air while her body had shaken and shivered and she screamed out her many years of withheld desires.

Marianne sighed and let a finger caress his shoulder. How much time she had wasted on the wrong man, how many years of sexual frustration she had dealt with being with a man who hardly wanted her.

The man in her bed opened his eyes slowly. Then he smiled. Marianne wanted to kiss him, but hesitated. After all they weren't

## Three, Four ... Better lock your door

lovers, they weren't even friends. He was just someone she had paid an escort company to send over and to have sex with her and her husband. She had always thought a threesome would spice their sex life up a little. Boy how it had. She had never imagined that he would only do her, though. But now she was kind of happy that it had all been about her.

She had asked him not to go in the bathroom to Martin. Told him that her husband didn't care about it. Then she had ordered him to do her again and again. Then she had fallen asleep, drained, exhausted, and happy. It was selfish. She knew that all too well. But she didn't want to share this guy with Martin. The very thought made her sick to her stomach. No he was hers, her pleasure, and her secret desire. Now she had to find some way to make it up to Martin today. He was probably angry with her. She realized she hoped he was. At least that would be something. At least he was reacting. The worst part about him being retired was the complete indifference towards her and their life that he had displayed. It was like he thought his life was over now that he didn't have his practice anymore. Now that he had given his patients to his son and let go of his old life.

Marianne couldn't believe that the handsome man was still there. She thought she had heard him leave during the night, but he was still there when she opened her eyes. Now he turned his back to her. "I'd better be going," he said.

She touched his arm. "Don't. Stay. Have a cup of coffee and some breakfast. It's the least I can do for you."

"That's awfully nice of you. But it is really time for me to go. I have a rule of not being too social with my clients," he said and sat up in the bed. He looked at her and examined her body. She smiled shyly. "Even if I really liked you."

He removed the cover and got up out of the bed. Marianne looked at him with hungry eyes. She wanted another turn, she wanted more. She patted the bed with her hand. "Come back here. I am not done with you."

The man laughed. Then he leaned over and kissed her forehead. "You're very nice, but this is strictly business for me. You hired me, remember? If you want more you'll have to call the agency and ask for me. They have my schedule."

He started putting on his pants while Marianne looked disappointedly at him. She hated to see him go. She didn't want this to end. She never wanted to go back to her reality.

Just before he left he turned and winked at her. "I hope to see you again soon," he said with that low humming voice of his, that smooth voice that could melt even the coldest of hearts.

Then he was gone.

Marianne Frandsen stayed in bed for another few minutes while she heard him walk down the stairs and out the front door. Then she sighed, closed her eyes and tried to bring back the pictures of her and him in the bed the night before. It had been intense. She would probably never be able to sleep with Martin again after this, she thought.

"Can't go back," she mumbled as she walked into the bathroom.

The shower was on and the curtain closed. "You're up early," she said and sat on the toilet. She received no answer. Martin was probably still angry; she thought and chuckled on the inside. She didn't care anymore. She didn't need him. If he wanted to be angry then that was his choice. She flushed and got up.

"I'm making breakfast in a few seconds. Do you want a soft boiled egg?"

Martin was still not answering her. It pissed her off. Okay, so he was entitled to be mad at her, but what about how he had been treating her the last few years? Sitting in that chair of his in silence, never answering when she spoke, never listening to what she said or doing what she told him to. What about that? She was entitled to something too; she was entitled to be angry too, to want something more out of life. She had the right to enjoy herself, to enjoy a little guilty pleasure. It was after all something they had both agreed to. So what if the beautiful man had found her more interesting than an old wrinkled man. So what? Was that so strange? She was a beautiful woman in the prime of her life and if he couldn't see that, if he refused to appreciate that, then maybe there was just nothing more for them to do here. Maybe it was after all time for both of them to move on.

Agitated she grabbed the shower curtain. "Now you listen to me you silly old man," she said with great authority in her voice while she pulled it aside.

Then she fell backwards and hit her back on the sink. She crawled like a crab on all four to the hallway while trying to scream, but no sound ever left her lips.

She tumbled down the stairs half crawling half running and falling. She gasped for air trying hard to let out a scream, a cry, a yell, even a shriek. But there were no loud sounds left in her. From that day on Marianne Frandsen could do nothing more than whisper even when she - like now - tried to scream at the top of her lungs.

## Chapter 31

JULIE HAD NIGHTMARES AGAIN THAT NIGHT AND SLEPT IN MY BED. I woke with a sore neck, growling and groaning. Julie kissed me.

"Come on, Mom. It's time to get up now."

Julie grabbed my arm and pulled me up.

"What are you so cheerful about this early?" I said.

"Today is my first riding lesson. I'm on the same team as Tobias down at the club."

I opened my eyes widely. "Excuse me? You're what?"

Julie froze. Then she sighed like only a child can sigh. "Grownups are so lame. Grandpa didn't tell you did he? He promised to take me today."

I shook my head. "I guess he forgot."

I walked downstairs planning on being very angry with Dad and his way of handling this. I had said no to my daughter and he wasn't supposed to just overrule that. Even my steps on the stairs were mad. But then I heard him whistle in the kitchen and the smell of bacon and eggs filled my nostrils I realized I couldn't be mad at him.

I walked into the kitchen. Dad turned and smiled. "Already up?" he asked. His cheeks were red from standing over the hot stove.

"Breakfast is almost ready."

I looked at the greasy bacon on the pan. It smelled really good and I was starving. I felt my jeans. They felt tight. I almost couldn't close them this morning. Then I thought about Christian and my plans to have dinner with him Wednesday night.

Dad swung the pan and put it on the table. "Bacon? I even went to the bakery and got pastries to go with it." He showed me a basket of delicious looking pastries.

"I think I'll just grab some granola this morning, Dad. But thanks," I said.

"Granola?" Julie entered the kitchen and looked at me with a little wrinkle in her forehead. "You never eat granola."

I grabbed a box of cereal with granola from the shelf and poured some into a bowl. "Well I do now," I said.

"That's weird," Julie said and sat down. Then she started shoveling pastries in one at a time while I watched her with great envy. I used to be able to do that too and never gain a single pound. It wasn't fair. My granola with milk was dry and boring. I washed it down with lots of orange juice.

"So Dad, Julie tells me that you're taking her to her first riding lesson today?" I said.

Julie crouched in her chair.

Dad froze. He stared at me. Then he threw up his hands. "I'm sorry sweetheart. I meant to tell you, I really did, but you just haven't been home much lately ... and I know that you've said no but I thought that it would be good for Julie ..."

"It's okay Dad. I know she can be persuasive and she has probably not stopped talking about it since we had this conversation the first time. I was mad at her at first for going behind my back but I'm over it. It's okay, really. As long as she's home before dark and as long as you keep an eye on her all the time. We have to be very careful these days, you know."

Julie smiled. She jumped out of her chair and smothered me in an amazing hug. "Thank you, thank you, thank you! You're the best mom ever."

I hugged her back. Then I looked into her eyes. "Just promise to be careful, alright? And always wear a helmet."

"I will."

"You're wearing make-up?"

Sune stared at me like I had just fallen off the moon. I blushed. I didn't think he would notice let alone comment on it.

"Can't a woman wear make-up every once in a while?" I asked and stormed past him to my desk.

"You never wear make-up," Sune continued.

"Well I do now, okay. Leave me alone."

He raised his hands in the air resignedly. "Okay," he said and walked back to his desk. "So what's on the menu today? What are we working on?"

I stared at the big pile of papers and files on the floor next to me. "We have to go through all this," I said. "I haven't talked to Jens-Ole about it yet since I want to make sure that the documentation is there. I want to make sure we actually have a story. He didn't want

## Three, Four ... Better lock your door

me to pursue this story in the first place and I don't want him to shoot it down because I'm not properly prepared."

The door to the editorial room suddenly opened and Sara stormed in. She was out of breath. "Another one ... there ... heard it ... in my car ..." she gasped.

"Take it easy Sara. Catch your breath first. Then talk nice and slow," I said.

"There's been another one. Another murder. All patrols are on their way there now. Just heard it in my car on my way here," she said.

Sune and I stared at each other. He grabbed his coat and camera.

"Do you have a police scanner in your car as well?" I asked.

She nodded still gasping for air. "It's on Lungshave, on Enoe, the nice and rich neighborhoods."

The small island of Enoe was connected to Karrebaeksminde by a long bridge. It was a place mostly for camping, for vacation houses and summer guests. But there were a few neighborhoods where people lived all year, mostly elderly, retired people, but often they were very rich and just wanted to retire in beautiful surroundings close to the beach.

I had come there a lot a few years ago when I dated the Italian artist. He lived in one of the charming old houses right at the beach. We passed it on our way to the scene. I sent him a friendly thought and wondered how he was doing. If I knew him he had already found someone else and didn't miss me at all.

"Do you ever miss him?" Sune asked when we passed the house.

"No. He was an idiot," I said. "Cute, but not worth it."

Sune made a grimace. "Okay then. I get the picture. I shouldn't be asking more about him."

"No it's not like that. I don't mind talking about it. I'm completely over him."

We both went quiet. I chuckled.

"What?" Sune asked.

"Nothing."

"You chuckled," he said smiling.

"I like this, talking to you, even if it is only when we're working. I know we were supposed to stay strictly professional, but it's nice to talk about other stuff every now and then. I enjoy it."

Sune smiled. "I do too." Then he sighed. It wasn't a nice sigh. It was a longing one. I felt his eyes on me. I went quiet. I liked that he was looking at me, but I didn't want to like it.

"Stop staring," I said. "It makes me uncomfortable."

He turned his head, blushing. "I'm sorry. It's just because you look really great today."

I exhaled. I had to end this. I had to make him stop longing for me. It would end up destroying our relationship.

"I'm going out for dinner tomorrow night," I said. "With a man. Not that it's any of your business, but I want you to know."

Sune froze. He stared out of the window for a while in silence. Then he spoke without looking at me. "So who is he? Who's the lucky guy?" His voice was thick with disappointment.

I cleared my throat. "Christian Lonstedt."

Sune turned his head and looked at me. "Christian from the *Express*?"

"Yes."

"You can't go out with him," Sune said.

"Excuse me?"

"He's from the other newspaper, our competitor. He just wants to steal your stories and your sources," Sune answered with a slightly desperate tone to his voice.

"Come on. This is not some movie. Who would ever go out with someone to get stories or secrets out of them?"

Sune exhaled. "I just don't like it. I don't like him."

The scene of the crime was ahead of us now. I could see the pack of police cars parked in front. I drove up and parked not far away from the house. I turned off the engine and looked at Sune.

"Sune. You've always liked Christian. You like him more than I do. You're only saying that out of jealousy. I am going out with him tomorrow night. We are going to have a nice time and if everything goes well we might end up seeing each other again. You need to find peace with that if we're supposed to work together, okay? I love you as a friend. I don't want to lose you. If you're jealous then keep it to yourself. It will pass. You'll find someone else. Can you do that? Can you restrain yourself?"

Sune exhaled. Then he nodded. "Alright. You're right. This was about to happen someday anyway. I just have to make peace with it."

"That's what I wanted to hear. Now let's get to work."

## Chapter 32

THE SCENE OF THE CRIME LOOKED MUCH LIKE THE THREE BEFORE IT. Lots of police were working behind the red and white crime tape, the blue van from the forensic department, and people in blue suits dusting, securing fingerprints and taking footprints on the ground outside of the house. Neighbors had gathered, staring at the scene with terrified eyes, wondering why of all the houses did the killer pick this one? Why of all victims did he pick this man?

The victim was a sixty-seven year old man, Johannes Lindstroem explained to me when he saw me. He was a retired doctor who had his own practice in Naestved for ten years. The doctor was known to be the quiet type, his family very calm and nice according to the neighbors.

"He was killed in the shower, bled to death after having gone through what appears to be a lobotomy performed with a scalpel."

"Like the other three," I said.

"Just like the others. The perpetrator leaves no fingerprints behind. We have however found a few more blond hairs at the scene close to the body, which leads us to believe that we are looking for a woman.

"Who found the body?" I asked.

"The wife. She found it in the shower this morning."

"Did something happen last night? Did the neighbors hear or see anything?" I asked. "Anything out of the extraordinary?"

"That's what we're trying to find out. The wife has been taken to the hospital in Naestved. She is in a state of shock and not of much help yet. She has somehow lost her voice and can only whisper. What we have gotten out of her so far has led us nowhere, mostly mumbling and a few words here and there. The fact is we have no idea what has gone on here. Other than she woke up this morning went to the bathroom and found her husband."

"Okay, thanks," I said and let him get back to his work. Sune danced around the scene and taking pictures needed. I approached him.

"Anything good?" he asked while still shooting.

"They don't know much. The wife is in shock. But it's the same killer alright. Same methods, they even found more blond hair, so they're pretty sure they're looking for a blond woman."

"Hmm," Sune said while checking the last picture he had taken.

"What?" I asked.

"Isn't it weird that someone who leaves no fingerprints on the scene isn't careful enough to not leave hair behind?"

I nodded pensively. "I guess. So you're thinking that maybe someone wants us to think that it is a blond woman?"

Sune shrugged. "Just a thought."

"Hi there." Christian Lonstedt approached us. He had his camera around his neck and a notepad in the hand. He looked great.

I smiled. Sune scoffed and shook his head.

"Hi Christian," I said feeling a little awkward thinking about our upcoming dinner plans. He gave me a quick kiss on the cheek. Sune continued taking pictures.

"So one more, huh? This is really ugly," Christian said. "Makes you kind of afraid to go out at night."

"Except half of them have been killed in their homes," Sune growled. "So my guess is going out would be the safe thing to do."

He had a point, I thought to myself.

"Unless the killer picks her victims while they're out and then follows them home," Christian argued.

He made a good point as well, I thought. Maybe it was as simple as that. Maybe the victims were coincidental? It didn't seem like the good Dr. Martin Frandsen had engaged himself in anything particularly morally wrong like the three others. Maybe our theory was as farfetched as it sounded?

"Well I'd better get back to work. I have to get back and write the article," Christian said. "See you tomorrow. I'll pick you up at six."

Sune and I stayed till the body had left the house in a body bag and then we headed back to the editorial room in Karrebaeksminde. Sune was awfully quiet all the way back but I let him sulk all he wanted to while I tried to keep myself joyful and happy.

"Don't you ever wonder how he gets there so fast?" Sune said when we had crossed the bridge and drove back towards town.

"Who Christian?"

"Yes. He is always there when we arrive."

## Three, Four ... Better lock your door

I shrugged. "My guess is that he has a police scanner in his home just like Sara."

"But he has to go all the way from Naestved?"

I shrugged again. "Today he didn't. Today he didn't come until after we were there. Maybe he is just a really good reporter."

"Maybe he doesn't have a life."

I scoffed while I drove the car to our usual parking lot near the office. "Let it go, will you?" I said. "I like him and you have to accept that."

We bought lunch at a small café that we passed on the way and brought the sandwiches up to the editorial room. Sune didn't speak to me at all and avoided my eyes. It was getting on my nerves, it was so childish and for the first time I felt how young he really was compared to me. It was also very unattractive.

Sara sensed the tension right away and shook her head. "I told you you were heading for trouble," she mumbled.

I ignored her. I wrote a couple of articles about the new killing while finishing my lunch. Then I sent it to my editor. He e-mailed me back that it looked great. He especially loved the portrait of the retired doctor. I had talked to a bunch of neighbors and Googled Martin Frandsen. In my article I painted a picture of a respectable hardworking man who was very well-liked in his community and by his patients.

"It shows that anybody could be the next victim," my editor wrote.

I went for coffee in the kitchen. I came back with a cup for Sune and placed it on his desk.

"Thanks," he mumbled.

"You're welcome," I said and went back to my desk.

"There is cake too," Sara said. "Cinnamon stick, your favorite."

"I saw it but I'm skipping cake today," I said and tapped my belly.

Sune scoffed. "She has a date tomorrow," he said.

"It's not a date!" I exclaimed. "Just two friends having dinner." I sat down and sipped my coffee ignoring him. Sara looked at me with curious eyes.

"So who is he?" she asked.

"I don't think you know him," I said.

"But I might. At least tell me his name."

I sighed. Why were they insisting on making a big deal out of this? "His name is Christian Lonstedt. He works for the *Express*. He's just a colleague and new to this area. It's nothing really. He's just lonely and needs to get out a little."

Sara nodded pensively. "Don't think I've ever heard of him."

My cell phone started ringing on the table. I leaned over to grab it. "Well like I said, he is new to the area," I said and picked up the phone. It was my dad. "Hi Dad, what's up?"

"It's Julie. You need to come. She's in the hospital in Naestved. She fell off the horse and hurt herself."

My heart dropped. "Is she alright?"

"Yes," Dad said. "But you better come."

"Of course. I'll be right there."

I was about to hang up when Dad stopped me. "Tell Sune I have Tobias with me here. He wanted to go with Julie in the ambulance. He didn't want to leave her side."

"Okay. Be there as soon as possible," I said and hung up.

"What's going on?" Sune asked.

I grabbed my coat from behind my chair and took my phone and bag. "We're going to Naestved," I said. "I'll explain on our way there."

## Chapter 33

DAD LOOKED TIRED AND CONFUSED WHEN I RAN TOWARDS HIM IN THE emergency-room at the hospital. I had broken all traffic-laws including running several red lights to get there as fast as I could. Twelve minutes later I was hugging my dad in the hallway outside her room. Tobias ran towards Sune.

"How is she?" I asked. My hands were shaking.

"She's fine," Dad said. "She fell off the horse and broke her wrist."

"I knew it. I knew I shouldn't have let her ride those beasts. It's way too dangerous for a small girl like her."

"It wasn't the horse's fault," exclaimed Tobias suddenly. "Someone was mean to it!"

"Tobias!" Sune hushed at his son.

I looked at Dad. "He's right. It wasn't the horse's fault, nor was it Julie's," he said.

I was confused. "What are you saying, Dad?"

"You'd better sit down while I explain," he said.

I sat in a green chair, Dad and Sune sat next to me. Sune gave Tobias some change coin to go get a soda from the machine.

Dad sighed and shook his head. "If only I had been faster this wouldn't have happened. It's this stupid cane!" He slammed the cane in the floor. "I tried to run for her, I tried to run to help her, but I couldn't. I was too slow."

I grabbed his hand. "It's okay, Dad. Nobody's blaming you for anything. Just tell me what happened. From the beginning, please."

"Well I picked up Tobias and Julie after school like we had planned and drove them to the club a little outside of town where Tobias usually takes his riding-lessons. Everything was great, I mean the kids were having fun, enjoying being together again outside of school and we were all singing in the car. When we arrived at the club Julie borrowed a helmet and a horse and the lesson began. All the students were riding in circles in the outdoor riding arena. Julie was picking it up so fast I was really proud of her. I took a lot of pictures with my stupid phone. I guess I wasn't paying attention for a second or two, I was having trouble with this damn thing and the camera, but when I lifted the phone to take another picture I saw that Julie had stopped. She was talking to someone by the fence. The guy was giving the horse a carrot and talked to her."

"What guy? Was it someone she knew? What did he look like?" I asked.

"I never came close enough to take a good look at him before he was gone, but he was wearing a black suit and tie underneath a long black coat. I remember thinking that it was a strange way to be dressed in a place like this."

I looked at Sune then at Dad. I was so confused. What was this? "Why was he talking to Julie?"

"According to what she told me, he said that he knew you. He knew the journalist Rebekka Franck. He wanted Julie to deliver a message to you."

I felt a wave of anger build up inside of me. "A message. What message? Who was this guy?"

"He wanted Julie to tell you that he knew everything about you. He knew where you lived and you were working on a new story. He said it would be worse for you if you didn't back out, if you didn't drop the story."

"What would be worse for me? If I didn't back out from what? I don't get it. What is this supposed to be? Some kind of threat? Do they think this is some kind of mobster-gangster movie or something?"

My dad sighed and put his hand on top of mine. "Sweetie. He threatened your family, your daughter. Are you working on some story that could endanger you or Julie?"

I could literally hear the blood pumping through my veins. I was so angry I could explode. Who the hell did this guy think he was?

"Then what happened? How did Julie hurt herself?" Sune asked.

"Well, as soon as I saw this guy talking to Julie I knew I had to go and see who he was and find out why he was talking to my granddaughter. So I started running, but I couldn't make it in time to stop him."

"Stop him from doing what? What did he do to my daughter?" I asked with desperate voice. This was freaking me out.

"He had a whip of some sort in his hand and as soon as he told Julie to deliver the message to you he raised the whip and hit the horse in the face. The horse was naturally scared and it balked with Julie screaming and holding on to the saddle. Then it took off. It started running through the arena and eventually jumped the fence. The riding instructor was yelling and calling but it was too late. It ran towards the forest with Julie on its back. She fell off it inside of the forest and broke her wrist when she hit the ground. Her head hit a big rock." Dad showed me the helmet. The back was cracked open. "The helmet broke but luckily Julie's head is still intact."

I looked at the cracked helmet. "This could have been Julie's head," I said startled, alarmed to the point of a possible meltdown.

"Thank God she was wearing a helmet," Sune said.

I leaned back in my chair with a sigh. The story the man had been referring to had to be the story about the lobotomies done in the nineties. This was a serious threat to make me not run the story. These guys meant business. They could have killed Julie.

"Can I see her?"

"Sure. They will keep her for the night to make sure her head hasn't suffered any damage, but so far they say that it looks perfectly normal. She suffered a blow to the head though and we need to keep an eye on that. If she starts to throw up or something like that in the next couple of days."

"Sure," I said and got up from my chair. I didn't know whether to cry or be angry. So I chose to do neither. In a state of paralyzed shock I went into Julie's room.

She was sitting in her bed and smiling so sweetly when I entered. Her blue eyes stared at me.

"I'm okay Mom. Don't worry," she started. "Please don't be mad at Granddad."

I smiled and walked towards her. Her arm already had a cast on. "I'm not mad, sweetie," I said and sat on her bed. Then I hugged her for a long time until she pulled away from me.

"Mom, I just fell off the horse. It was really nothing. They say you have to fall off a hundred times before you're a real rider."

I laughed and touched her cast. "I guess we'll have to have all of your friends over to sign this thing, huh?"

She nodded. "I guess."

Then she went quiet, pensive for a moment before she spoke again: "Mom who was that man?"

I shook my head. "I don't know sweetie. I wish I did."

"He was really nice to begin with, but then he did that thing with the whip. Why did he do that?"

"I don't know that either sweetie. My guess is that he wanted to scare me. That's why he tried to get to you and give you the message instead of telling me himself. He wanted me to be afraid that something might happen to you if I didn't do what he told me to. He knows that you mean the world to me and I would never let anything happen to you."

"So you're not doing the story?" She looked at me with discontent.

"I don't think so," I said. "It's not worth it if anything happens to you. I won't risk it."

"Then he won," she said.

I exhaled deeply knowing that she was right.

"Mrs. Lejrskov, our teacher always says that if we don't tell on a bully then he'll just bully someone else."

I chuckled. "Well she is very wise. But this is a little more than bullying. Now get some rest, you hurt your head so you need it. I'll be right outside the door with Granddad and Tobias."

Julie put her head on her pillow with a smile. "I love you Mom," she mumbled just before I exited the room.

## Chapter 34

I stayed at the hospital with Julie all night and brought her home the next morning after the doctor had checked up on her and assured me that everything looked fine and normal. She could even go to school the very next day if she wanted to, he said.

I called Jens-Ole from my car and told him I wasn't going to come in that day, that I needed to spend time with my family. Luckily he understood. I didn't tell him about the story or the reason for Julie's accident. I guess I was afraid that he would be mad at me for hiding the story from him or for going ahead with a story he had clearly asked me to drop.

Julie was tired but glad to be able to spend an entire day with her mother. I turned off the phone and Julie found an old puzzle with three thousand pieces that she wanted to do with me and her granddad. My dad made coffee and hot chocolate and we sat by the kitchen table for hours and hours putting the pieces in their right places, trying to create the beautiful mountain picture that was shown on the box. We laughed and talked about everything and nothing. It felt good and I really enjoyed it. My stress level went down immediately and I found myself not thinking about work for once. Julie who only had one hand to work on the puzzle seemed happier than I had seen her in a long time.

It was what we all needed.

Later Julie and I took a nap together on the couch while Dad watched some program about gardening on TV. When I woke up it was almost six o'clock.

"Dinner," I mumbled. I had completely forgotten about my dinner with Christian. I looked at Julie. Her head was in my lap. She stretched herself and yawned. I had to cancel it, I thought. I couldn't leave her now. Not when she was this vulnerable and needed her mother the most.

"Weren't you supposed to go out tonight?" Dad asked.

I shook my head and caressed Julie's head. "I'm not going."

Julie sat up on the couch. "Why?"

I sighed. "Because I can't. You need me here."

Julie tilted her head and looked at me with her blue eyes. "Mom. We have been together all day. I'll be going to bed in like two hours. I think I'll be fine without you until then. Grandpa and I will do something fun, right?" She looked at him and he nodded.

"Sure," he said. "We always have fun."

"Are you sure it's alright?" I looked at their faces waiting for one of them to tell me it wasn't going to be alright, that they needed me here. I badly wanted them to need me; I really wasn't in the mood to go out and especially not in the mood to leave Julie. I wanted to be there to protect her should anything happen to her again. To my disappointment they both nodded.

Julie got up from the couch. "I'll help you find something nice to wear." She started walking up the stairs. I stared at her. I really didn't want to go.

"You can't keep an eye on her forever anyway," Dad said.

I chuckled softly knowing perfectly well that he was right. I needed to be able to live my life and let Julie live her life. It was just so difficult to let go.

Christian knocked at the door at precisely six o'clock. Julie ran to open it. I followed her down the stairs and came up behind her in the open door.

"Hi, I'm Julie," she said and reached out her hand.

Christian looked a little perplexed and I felt a pinch in my stomach. I hadn't told him that I had a daughter yet and suddenly I was afraid of his reaction. I wondered if he would react anything like Giovanni, the Italian artist I had dated.

Christian smiled charmingly and then he shook her hand. "Well hello there," he said. "Have you been helping your mom get ready?"

Julie nodded eagerly.

"I thought so. I think you did an amazing job with her," he said. "She looks gorgeous."

Julie was one huge smile. So was I. Finally, a guy who knew how to talk to my daughter. Finally someone who didn't consider children as something that should be "seen and not heard." So far so good, I thought.

"Look Mom. He brought you flowers!" Julie said.

Christian pulled out a bouquet he had been hiding behind his back. "Actually they're for you little angel," he said and winked at me while he handed them to Julie. She laughed that sweet childlike laughter of hers.

"You'd better put them in water before they die, sweetie," I said.

"Sure" she turned around and was about to walk away.

"What do you say?" I asked.

She smiled at Christian. "Thank you," she said. "Thank you so much."

He bowed lightly with a pleasant smile. "You're very welcome."

"I like him, Mom," she said just before she ran towards the kitchen with the bouquet in her hands.

"Sorry about that," I said.

Christian shook his head. "No. Don't be. She's wonderful."

"I meant I was sorry I didn't tell you I had a daughter," I said.

"I knew that," he said.

"Oh. I just figured that since I hadn't told you that you didn't know."

"I'm a journalist, remember? I do research," he said with a grin. "How do you think I figured out where you lived?" He reached out his hand. "Shall we?"

I grabbed my jacket from a hanger in the closet right behind the entrance door and put it on. Then I yelled to Dad and Julie that I was leaving and closed the door behind me. He was still holding his hand out toward me. I took it. It felt weird holding someone's hand again. Other than Julie I hadn't held hands with anyone in years. Peter and I never did it much and after we had Julie it kind of stopped. It made me feel like a teenager again. It was odd but enthralling. I guess I enjoyed it.

"I've never dated another journalist before," I said. "I guess I can't have many secrets."

Christian looked at me. I was so attracted to him at that moment. He seemed so vulnerable, so sad and yet so strong.

"Or maybe that's what I like about you," he said. "Your mysteriousness. You have an aura of mystery surrounding you."

I laughed loudly. "I was just thinking that same thing about you. I can't quite put my finger on it. It's like you're somehow too perfect."

"Then I guess we're the perfect match."

I laughed again and so did he.

We took a cab to the restaurant. Christian had reserved a table at Brohjoernet - which was an old family-owned restaurant right on the water that served old-fashioned Danish dishes like roasted pork with potatoes and parsley sauce or chopped steak with fried onions. The building was from around 1820 situated with views over the waters and Enoe in the distance. We sat at a table by the window and enjoyed the glistening lights from the cars crossing the bridge to the island. It was dark outside but the many lights from houses and cars on Enoe made the view spectacular. It was like the night was on fire.

I had a steak while Christian had the roasted pork. We didn't find it hard to talk to one another like I usually did on a first date. On the contrary we talked so much we hardly had time to eat. Christian made me laugh. He was charming and funny and he had a twinkle in his eye when he spoke. He was passionate about his work and especially about his time in Zimbabwe. He liked being there, he liked it even more so than being in Denmark, he said.

"It was hard to get back."

"Why?" I sipped my wine.

"Because it is so different here. No one is starving, everybody has everything and they don't even know how to appreciate it. Once you've tried living in a place where there is need and once you've tried what it is like to be able to help these people, to live for others instead of just yourself, then you can't go back. It was the most fulfilling yet the most frustrating time I have ever had. But I'd rather have that than living here where everything is status quo. Where there is nothing at stake. Plus it's really cold here compared to there."

I laughed. "I know. I've always dreamt about doing what you've done. Go out into the world and experience what it is like. I would love to help people like that. To hand them food or help them build a school."

Christian drank from his glass. His eyes were serious, passionate. "It was quite fulfilling. But also frustrating because you can't help everybody. The need is so huge that you can hardly comprehend it. I came there as a journalist expecting to do the organization's newsletter, website and basically help spread the word about what they do in order to raise more money but I ended up doing everything else too. By the end I was also a handyman, a schoolteacher and a nurse."

I ate some of my steak thinking how I was wasting my life making no difference in this world to anyone. But it was hard to go out in the world when you had a child who needed education and a stable environment. When I had been a war-correspondent in Iraq I had somehow felt that I was making a difference. I was telling important stories about how the Danish soldiers were helping the population, how they were changing their lives and how they were fighting to get democracy, something we took so terribly for granted in our daily lives. I had found my job there extremely fulfilling. But then I had Julie and now I was here.

Democracy, I thought and tasted the word while my eyes wandered in the room. Wasn't it my job as a reporter to protect it? Wasn't it my duty to tell the Danish population when power was misused by politicians? I sighed and looked at Christian while he was

## Three, Four ... Better lock your door

talking about Africa while gesturing with his hands. I needed this kind of passion back in my life.

But was I willing to pay the price?

I didn't know. Julie was my whole life now. I had to protect her before anything else.

"You're so quiet all of a sudden," Christian said.

I smiled. "It's just been a busy couple of days lately. It's nice to do something else than work for a change."

Christian smiled and nodded. "I know what you mean."

"I bet you do. It can probably get hectic at the *Express* every now and then," I said. I emptied my glass of wine. Christian poured more in it. I was getting tipsy, but let it happen. I wanted to be relaxed and enjoy this moment. This was a nice restaurant and a nice guy that I was getting more and more attracted to as the night progressed. He kept ordering more wine and little by little I let my guard completely down. I told him about my ex-husband, how we met, how we had grown apart, how he had developed mental issues after coming back from war, how he had become more and more sick as the months passed and how I finally had to leave him in order to protect my daughter.

"That must have been tough on Julie?" Christian asked.

I smiled. I loved that he thought about her before me. I nodded. "It was. She was still pretty young so she didn't understand much of it, but she missed him a lot. Still does."

"So where is he now?"

I shrugged. "Haven't heard from him in two years. He probably left the country to go God knows where. Like you he found it hard to come back. He was an adrenalin junkie. So he kept going back."

"That's really sad," Christian said. "He had everything. A beautiful wife and a wonderful daughter. I don't get people who throw away everything like that. What I wouldn't give to have what he had."

"You're a family man?" I asked surprised. He kept amazing me. He was nothing like I had first taken him for.

"I always wanted a family."

"So why don't you?"

"Well, it just never happened. I'm thirty-seven and I'm still alone," he said. "I guess I made some stupid choices along the way. I thought it would happen eventually, but it never did."

"Haven't you been close? Like engaged to be married or something?" I asked while the waiter brought my dessert. Apple pie with whipped cream. I didn't even think about it twice before I dug in.

"There have been a few," he said while I ate, "but never anything really serious. I think I have been too involved in my work to really be able to devote myself fully to a relationship."

The warm apple pie tasted heavenly. I drank some wine. Then I looked at him. His eyes had a sadness to them.

"My parents died when my sister and I were only eight," he said. "I guess I find it hard to be close to anyone. I'm too afraid to lose them."

I smiled and put my hand on top of his. The touch made my skin shiver. He had never looked so attractive than he did at this vulnerable moment.

"So you're twins? You and your sister?" I asked. "You said you were both eight when they died."

Christian nodded. "Yes. Yes we are."

"That's nice." I sipped more wine and felt a little dizzy now. Christian smiled his charming smile and I suddenly felt an urge to kiss him.

"So who do you think is the killer?" he suddenly asked me.

"The lobotomy killer? I don't know. But I have a feeling that someone really wants us to think that it's a blond woman."

Christian became serious. "Why would you say that?"

"Wait. Are you only asking because you want a story for your paper?" I asked.

"You got me," he said. "I guess I only took you to dinner to pump you for inside information." He looked at me.

I felt bad. "I'm sorry," I said. "Like I said. I'm not used to dating other journalists."

He smiled. "Well I'll forgive you." He paused. "I was only interested in your opinion. Nothing else. Just making conversation."

"Okay. But if you really want to know then I think it's weird that the killer makes an effort not to leave any fingerprints behind but the last couple of killings they have found hair, long blond hair. It's a little too strange, if you ask me. Too obvious."

Christian nodded. "You make a good point. But couldn't it just be a coincidence?"

"I don't know. Luckily it's not my job to catch the killer only to write about it and hopefully one day write the article about who it was."

Christian looked at me. Then he lifted his glass and made a toast. "To leaving it to the police to catch the lobotomy killer," he said as our glass touched.

Christian paid for dinner and we started walking along the canal. Huge wooden fishing boats were in the water waiting for dawn to arrive and another work-day to begin.

"There is something that has caused me to wonder about you," I said.

"And that is?"

## Three, Four ... Better lock your door

I looked at him. He smiled again. I adored that smile. "How come you're always so fast to get at the scene of crime? You're always there before me."

Christian laughed. "And I bet you don't like that."

I shook my head. "No, I really don't."

"You're so competitive. Can't stand to lose, can you?"

I chuckled. "I know. It's bad isn't it?"

"A little," he said. "Not your most attractive side."

"But I really don't understand how you can get there so fast from Naestved?"

He paused. He looked at me. "Why Naestved?" he asked. "Ah, I get it. You think I live in Naestved, don't you? Just because I work there."

"Don't you? It would be the sensible place to live. Close to work and everything."

"Sure. But I don't. As a matter of fact I live not far from here. Right up that street up there and to your right."

I laughed. "That makes more sense," I said. "So you must have a police scanner just like we do?"

He smiled. "Yes. You got me. You didn't invent it you know. Many journalists and freelance photographers own them."

"I know." I paused again. "Say how come I haven't seen your name on any of the bylines in the paper yet?" I asked.

Christian smiled and chuckled.

I nodded. "I get it," I said. "Just like Frederik to take credit for the stories himself. He is the laziest journalist I have ever met. Can you believe he never shows up to anything around here? He just writes the stories often based on tips from people calling in or news-telegrams. I know he hates being stuck out here in the countryside writing stories he doesn't think matter to anyone. I bet he makes you do all the work now, huh? That would suit him perfectly fine."

Christian scoffed. "Well it sounds like you know him," he said.

We both walked on in silence. I felt his hand in mine. I leaned on his shoulder. "This is nice," I said.

He stopped. I felt his hand under my chin. He lifted it gently. Then I felt his lips on mine. I closed my eyes. His lips were so soft. His kiss made my skin shiver. I kissed him back. Gently, awaiting, luring him in. Then he became demanding, insisting. He held my face between his hands while he kissed my face, my neck, and my ears. He moaned in my ear, whispered under his breath.

"I want you badly. I want to be inside of you. I've wanted it since the first time we met."

I touched his face while taking my decision. He was shaking. Then I kissed him.

"Let's go to your place," I said when our lips parted.

## Chapter 35

SHE WATCHED THEM ALL NIGHT. WATCHED THIS NICE COUPLE OUT ON their first date together. The woman was sitting right behind them in the restaurant overlooking the water. She watched them eat and drink and listened in on their conversation. She couldn't help it. They were so sweet, so horrifically nice. They talked about all kinds of things. They got to know each other really well. He talked about living in Africa and helping children while working for some organization out there. It was so nice, the woman watching thought to herself. The way he cared for other people. That was really admirable.

The woman looked delicate in her dress that she told him her daughter had picked out for her. She was truly a beauty and he was quite the catch as well.

They ate and drank wine till their cheeks turned reddish. Then the man paid the bill, like the gentleman he was, and they left the restaurant amicably chatting and laughing.

The woman followed them as they walked along the canal. They were chatting, holding hands and then they stopped and to her great joy they finally shared their first kiss. She watched them from a distance while they were suddenly all over each other. She enjoyed the desire, the lust that surrounded them. She lived for it, she craved it.

It made her want to kill.

But she had to restrain herself standing there by the canal. This wasn't the time or the place. Her time would come soon, she thought as she followed them up the street towards his apartment. She felt like clapping her hands with excitement as she saw them walk inside the building without locking the door. This was almost too easy. What a pity, she thought. Such nice people.

## Three, Four ... Better lock your door

She followed them up the stairs as they stopped to kiss again. It made her smile and giggle on the inside with pure joy. Oh the expectation of what was about to happen. Oh the pleasure this was going to give her.

The man opened the door to the apartment and their lips hardly moved away from each other as they walked through it. The woman giggled and followed them inside. Then she locked the door behind her while she heard them moan and groan in the bedroom where they were already undressing each other, throwing their clothes on the floor. It was almost unbearably arousing and thrilling for her to watch.

The man was sucking on the pretty woman's breasts and drinking from her lips. He was whispering dirty words in her ears that the woman watching could hardly hear but she knew them all too well. They were all the same. They were moaning and groaning the same words. It was disgusting, but also highly exciting to the woman in the hallway peeking in through the bedroom door that was slightly ajar.

The man was penetrating the woman now and she was moaning with desire, crying out for more and more, wanting him to keep on, go faster, do it harder. The woman watching felt a shiver go down her back, the shiver of extreme pleasure.

The sound of the bodies slamming against each other, the cries from the woman as she neared climax, the wildness of the man, the muscles moving, the sweat that caused their skin to glisten. He became wilder and more demanding. He was riding her now. Holding her hair while entering her, wilder and harder.

Then he exploded inside of her with a scream while the woman screamed out her pleasure and came at the same time.

The woman watching had to bite her hand to not scream as well and thereby reveal her presence.

When they were done with their act they lay on the bed, still sweating and panting. The woman watching saw them kissing and felt disgust. All that affection meant nothing to her. She liked to watch the act, the raw and pure sex.

Knowing that first act of the spectacle was over she sneaked into the bathroom and crawled into the shower. Ready for the next act she pulled the curtain. In her hand she held her scalpel tight. The other hand covered her mouth so no one would hear her giggling.

## Chapter 36

"That was really good," I said gasping for air.

We were lying on Christian's bed trying to catch our breath. Making love to him was incredible, I thought. So passionate, so wild, so ... I ran a finger down his chest. He was perfect. Almost too perfect, I thought. Muscular upper arms, broad chest and big hands. Oh how I adored a man with big hands. I loved it when they could cover mine. And Christian had strong hands. Big, strong hands.

He lifted one of them and let it caress my hair. I felt good at that moment. I didn't think about work or even Julie. It was the most relaxed I had been in years.

"Do you want more?" he whispered.

"Wow. Already ready for more? You're in a good shape," I said laughing. "I'm still exhausted."

"I have been known to have that effect on women," he said with a grin.

I exhaled. Then I grabbed his face and pulled it close to mine. I felt his heavy breath on my face. It smelled good. Everything about him smelled so good. His skin, his hair, even his breath I couldn't believe it. I kissed him to make sure he was real. His lips felt very real. He climbed on top of me while laughing. He held me down with his strong hands.

"Gotcha now," he said still grinning. "You can't run."

I laughed. "I'm not going anywhere," I said.

He paused. Then he became serious. He stared at me.

"What?" I asked. "Did I say something?"

His right eye winked three times before he returned to me. He shook his head. "Sorry," he said.

## Three, Four ... Better lock your door

"Where did you go all of a sudden? You became so distant?" I asked.

He rolled off me and lay next to me on the pillow. We both stared at the ceiling above. "I was just thinking about my sister, sorry."

"Now there's a turn off," I said.

"I know. I didn't mean to. She can just be really controlling you know. She would really resent me if she knew I slept with you on our first date. I could just suddenly hear her, hear what she would say."

"Like what?" I asked.

"Like 'You really blew it' and 'You can't do anything right' or 'She will never stay with you. She'll never be with a guy like you.' Stuff like that." He lifted his head and looked at me. "Don't tell me she's right. Don't tell me that you'll leave after this and I'll never see you again."

I shook my head. Then I touched his face gently. "Sweet, sweet Christian. Of course I would like to see you again. Sleeping with you means I trust you, it means I want to be with you, I want to get to know you more."

Christian exhaled deeply. "Boy am I glad to hear that," he said.

"You shouldn't listen to your sister," I said. "Sounds like she doesn't know what she's talking about. To be frank it doesn't sound like she treats you very nice."

"Well we're twins you know. We can be a little harsh to each other. It's no big deal. It's just that sometimes she gets to me, you know?"

"Sounds really dominant," I said.

"Yeah she can be. Always meddling in my life, telling me what to do. Says it's for my own good, but I get so tired of her." Christian shook his head.

"Sounds a little like my mother," I said and chuckled. "It was like she had nothing better to do than to call me up and tell me all the things that were wrong with me."

Christian looked at me and smiled. "Yes. Exactly like that. You'd think she had enough to do living her own life, right? Why does she have to meddle in mine?"

I kissed Christian on his lips. He tasted so incredible. Then I looked deep into his eyes. Those deep blue eyes. It was like staring into eternity.

"You'll just have to tell her off," I said. "Tell her to stay out of your life. Tell her you can take care of yourself perfectly fine and she has no business meddling."

"You really think that'll work?" he asked.

"Trust me," I said. "I've been through it with both my mother and my sister."

Christian smiled and kissed my forehead. Then he got up. "Do you want a beer or something?" he asked.

"I'll take something, if something is a glass of red wine," I said.

Christian smiled his beautiful smile. "Coming right up. I also have some crackers and cheese," he said and got up. "I'll just take a quick shower first."

## Chapter 37

He was alone when he entered the bathroom. The woman watching had butterflies in her stomach when she saw the handle turn and heard him come in. This was it. Now the time had come, finally her hour had arrived. The man closed the door and locked it behind him. The woman watching stared at him while he looked at himself in the mirror and splashed water in his face. He sighed and shook his head slowly like he was in disbelief, like he couldn't comprehend what he was seeing in the mirror.

The woman watched him. He was standing with his head bowed. He dried his face with a towel. The smell of sex was still on his skin.

The woman crept up behind him silently like a snake creeps up on its victim. She held the scalpel tightly in her hand.

"I can't do it," he mumbled and covered his face with his hands.

She smiled then she put her lips close to his ear.

"You have to," she whispered. "You know you have to do it." She placed the scalpel in his hand. "She knows too much already."

The man looked at himself in the mirror. He was standing with the scalpel raised in his hand. Then he threw it in the sink.

"Don't you understand anything?" he yelled. "This is a good thing in my life for once. You always destroy everything good in my life!"

"Shh," the woman hushed with a gentle voice. "She'll hear you."

The man exhaled deeply. "I like her. I really like this one."

The woman scoffed. She wasn't used to this kind of reluctant behavior from her brother. Usually he just did as he was told. But she could manage it. He would cave in eventually. After all she knew him better than he knew himself.

"What does that have to do with anything?" she said. "The only reason you went out with her was to figure out how much she knew.

That was the plan. To keep her close so she wouldn't find out about us. She is too dangerous for us right now. She knows way too much. Besides you're falling for her and I can't have that. You'll lose your focus."

The man struck his hand hard on the edge of the sink. "I won't do it!"

"But you have to dear brother," the woman said hissing. "You don't have a choice, remember?"

The man stared at his sister in the mirror. Her mouth moved when his did. The reflection told him that he had to do it, persuaded him with her soft yet persistent words. She had a way of dealing with her brother; she knew exactly how to make him do what she wanted him to. And they both knew she would get her way ultimately.

"I want you out of my life," he said trying his new approach. "I want you to stay out of my life!"

But the sister wouldn't hear of it. He could yell all he wanted to. The brother realized it now. She was never going to go away. She had overtaken him, taken over his body and his mind. She used him whenever she needed him to do something for her. She had reduced him to nothing more than a puppet. A marionette. And she wasn't going to stop until the mission was completed. But even then he wasn't even sure he would be able to get rid of her.

"Please just leave me alone," he pleaded crying. "I think this girl could be the one. I really like her."

The woman in the mirror giggled at him. That annoying giggling laughter filled with self-righteousness and condescension. He hated that sound so much. It was always there wasn't it? He couldn't escape it no matter how badly he wanted to. No matter how hard he tried. No matter how many doctors he consulted to help him. It would always be there. She would always be there, right there looking at him in the mirror, giggling, laughing at him, and ridiculing him.

He would have killed her right there in the bathroom in an instant. He would have slit her throat with the scalpel and freed himself of her endless tyranny.

If only she wasn't already dead.

## Chapter 38

CHRISTIAN TOOK FOREVER IN THE SHOWER. I THOUGHT I HEARD voices so I got up from the bed and walked to the bathroom door. I knocked.

"Christian. Is everything alright in there?"

It went quiet.

"Are you alright?" I asked again.

"Sure," his voice said. Then there was a fumbling by the door and he opened it slightly and peeked out. He looked confused. His left eye had tics.

"I thought I heard voices," I said. "Who were you talking to?"

He smiled awkwardly and shook his head nervously. "Nobody. I was just singing, I guess."

I glanced inside of the bathroom through the door, but couldn't see anyone. "Oh. Okay," I said. "Do you mind if I go ahead and open the wine?"

He nodded in short sharp movements. "Not at all. Go ahead. You'll find everything in the kitchen."

He closed the door and I went back into the bedroom to find a shirt to cover me up. I was still naked but didn't want to wear my tight dress so I decided to find one of his shirts in his closet. I opened it and started going through his clothes. It didn't take too long before I froze completely. In there, behind all his blue and white shirts I found a dress. A long beautiful blue evening dress. I took it out. Why did he have a dress in his closet? Could it be his sister's? I held it up in front of me and looked at myself in the mirror thinking I would look great in it. It was kind of old-fashioned and the fabric told me that it was an old dress. Then it struck me. I had seen this dress somewhere before. I had seen it in the picture that Sune had taken from the scene of the first murder. There had been a woman standing out in the crowd. A tall blond woman wearing this same kind of blue dress.

I looked at it a second time in the mirror. Yes it was definitely the same. I had noticed it since it stood out, it wasn't a dress a woman would normally wear walking down the street in Karrebaeksminde. And she had been an unusual woman.

I chuckled and then froze. Could it have been Christian I had seen wearing this dress? I mean I had heard about men dressing up like women to live out a side of themselves that they couldn't normally share with their friends and families. It didn't have to mean that they were gay, and Christian certainly wasn't, I knew that much by now. Transsexualism was the word. Was that what Christian was? A transsexual? I chuckled again. I couldn't imagine him in this dress. Would I be able to live with a boyfriend who was a transsexual and every now and then took a stroll in the street dressed like a woman? I wasn't sure. I shook my head. Maybe I was jumping to conclusions here. I hurried up and put the dress back. I could be wrong; it could after all have been his sister I had seen. Maybe it was her dress and she had forgotten it here or something.

I found a shirt and put it on. I loved the way it covered my body. Christian was a big guy. I liked that. I really liked him. I put the dress all the way in the back so he wouldn't suspect that I had seen it. Then when I was about to close the closet-door I spotted something else. It made my heart drop. Something was sticking out on the top shelf. I grabbed it and pulled it down. It was a wig. A blond wig. I gasped for air. What was this?

I thought I heard the door to the bathroom open so I hurried and threw the wig back on the shelf. Then I closed the door and walked back to the bed. I had no idea what to think anymore, I thought. Maybe it was about time to go home.

I picked up my stockings and started putting them back on. Then I took off Christian's shirt while wondering what I should tell him. My daughter called? Some kind of emergency? I felt sad. I really liked him, but this was just a little too much right now. I had to have some time to myself and think. I sighed and sat at the bed. The dress felt tight. Probably from all the food I had eaten tonight.

Christian was very quiet in the bathroom. I couldn't even hear the water running. Maybe he was done showering. I exhaled. I had to come up with something to tell him. I decided to go with the "My daughter called and I have to go home to her" angle. It was plausible enough after all she had been through.

My eyes scanned the room while I waited. I spotted a book on the bedside table. I picked it up. *Under the Burning Sun* was the title. I turned it over and read the back cover. My heart stopped. Literally. The book was written by a journalist named Tue Hansen who had

## Three, Four ... Better lock your door

lived in Zimbabwe for three years while working for a humanitarian organization. The book was about his experiences and how he had seen an entire village burned to the ground and how the villagers had fled to a church thinking they would be safe there. The attackers had then let the Danish journalist watch as they burned the church to the ground with the people inside of it.

"To let us understand that anything we did in this country was in vain. We might as well go home, they said. We couldn't change Africa," the text read. I read the last part three times. Those were Christian's exact words. This story was exactly what he had told me, to the very detail, to the word. Even the part about the young boy that he had gotten close to and tried to adopt was in this book.

Was it all just a lie?

I threw the book on the bed. Then I lifted my head and gasped. Christian was standing in front of me. He was wearing blue eye shadow and red lipstick. In his hand he held a scalpel. He was staring at me. Then he began to giggle like a little girl.

I got up on my feet. "What are you doing? Christian?" My heart was racing in my chest now.

"Oh!" he said. "Now where are my manners? I haven't presented myself. My name is Victoria. I am Christian's twin sister."

"Christian. This is not funny. Please cut it out," I said trying to sound like I wasn't scared of him.

Christian giggled again. "See there is where we are very different Christian and I. He wouldn't think this was funny either, but I do. I find it hilarious." He lifted the scalpel and took another step closer to me. I backed up.

"Christian. I am going to go home now. I don't want to be a part of this."

"Oh. That's too bad. Because that's exactly what you're going to be. And I'll do the parting."

"Christian. You can't be serious. Did you kill all those people?" I asked. My voice was trembling slightly.

"Christian didn't," he smiled. "But I did. Christian doesn't have it in him like I do. He always was a soft boy. He doesn't get the thrill out of it like I do." Christian leaned over and whispered. "It doesn't turn him on like it does me."

I shook my head in disbelief. "You're sick," I said.

Christian laughed out loud. "That I am." He walked slowly around me with the scalpel in front of him. The lipstick had smeared onto his cheek. His eyes had tics. His facial expression was completely different from the Christian I knew. It was as if he had somehow changed into an entirely different person. I heard his breath next to my ear. The scalpel was now close to my forehead. I gasped as it touched my skin.

"Stop it Christian," I said. I grabbed his hand and tried to pull the scalpel away from my face. But he was too strong. He grabbed my neck and held me tight in his hand. I gasped for air. He whispered in my ear.

"The thing is that Christian is too weak. He will never be able to get by without me. He never could. I always have to come to his rescue. I have to protect him from this cruel world. He would be lost without me. I wanted him to take revenge for me, but even in that he failed. He couldn't do it without my help."

I gasped again. "Revenge for what?"

"Revenge for my death of course. They killed me, those bastards. They cut me open and left me to live like a vegetable. But he chickened out. Said he couldn't do it. So of course I had to step in and help him. It was just like when I wanted Christian to kill our parents for what they had done to us. He couldn't do it." Christian laughed. Then he hissed in my ear. "So I had to. I had to finish the pain."

"You killed your own parents?" I asked. I felt sweat break out on my forehead and upper lip. I could still see the scalpel; it was right outside of my eye now. His grip on my throat became tighter as he spoke.

"It's a long story. I'm afraid I don't have the time to take a trip down memory lane with you. I'm kind of busy with something else," he said chuckling.

I saw the scalpel lifted and felt it pinch my forehead. Then I was thrown on the bed. Christian was on top of me holding me down by the throat. I was choking, gasping for air.

"This might sting a little," he said and placed the scalpel just above my eyes. Having read about lobotomies and how they were performed I sobbed by the very thought of what was about to happen. I saw the pictures I had seen on the Internet and heard Dr. Irene Hoeg's words as she had described the procedure to me. Then I screamed all I could half-choked.

The grip on my throat tightened and I felt like I was about to slip out of consciousness when I heard a huge noise followed by yelling. I heard my name, footsteps, and then the heavy weight on top of me was lifted and the grip on my throat removed gone. I coughed heavily, gasping for air, before I finally managed to focus and see what was going on. Christian was on the floor, fighting with someone. The scalpel had fallen out of his hand. They were beating each other and slapping, fists hitting faces and bodies. I saw Christian's attacker.

It was Sune.

He took a fist to his jaw and fell to the ground. Then he received a blow to his stomach and landed, moaning. I sat up then kicked Christian under the chin with both of my legs causing him to tumble backwards into a dresser. Sune was on his feet again, groaning. His

## Three, Four ... Better lock your door

nose was bleeding profusely. He wiped it on his sleeve before he grabbed my hand while Christian tried to get back on his feet. We ran towards the door. Christian grabbed my foot and I fell on my face. I tried to kick my way out of his grip hitting his face, but he didn't let go. Sune pulled my arm. Then he flattened Christian with a kick to the face. I looked at Sune who grabbed my arm and pulled me up. Christian yelled and screamed while we stormed out the front door and down the stairs. Christian was fast on his feet again and followed us, yelling at us in the hallway. I jumped several steps at a time, right behind Sune.

Christian was still yelling as we slammed the door and ran into the night.

## Chapter 39

We jumped into a taxi and had it take us back to my house. We didn't utter a word to each other until we were back in my living room. I found us a couple of beers and some paper towels to put on Sune's nose to stop the bleeding.

"You're shaking," he said looking at my hands.

I exhaled. "I know. I can't seem to stop."

"We need to call the police," he said.

"I know." I sat on the couch next to him and drank from my beer. I was devastated. I watched Sune as he got up and found his cell phone in his pocket. I heard him speak to someone and tell them about the attack.

"They'll try and go there right away, but he's probably long gone," Sune said as he came back. He sat next to me and drank his beer. "He's too smart. They won't catch him tonight."

I sighed. Christian knew where I lived. "I know," I said with heavy heart thinking about my daughter.

"They'll be here soon to take your statement," Sune continued.

I nodded. "Naturally."

We didn't have to wait long before two officers were at the door. I invited them in and told them everything I knew. They noted it all and promised me that they would do everything in their power to find this guy. Then they thanked me and left the house. Sune handed me my beer once they were gone. We sat on the couch.

"How did you know?" I asked.

Sune smiled. "You're going to hate me for this."

"I have a feeling that I won't," I said.

"Well I didn't feel good about you dating this guy, you know that.

## Three, Four ... Better lock your door

So I did what any jealous guy would do," he said and drank from his beer.

"You ran a background check on him?"

Sune nodded. "It took me a couple of hours to convince myself that it was a good idea. I was afraid you would be mad at me if you found out. Once I had persuaded myself that it was in both of our interests it was pretty easy, really. I couldn't find one article written by him in the *Express* or in any other newspaper. I called the newspaper in Naestved and the receptionist said they had never heard of him. Then I searched for him in Danida's database and no one by his name had ever worked there or been in Zimbabwe working for them."

"He had the story from a book," I said. "Can't believe I let him fool me like that."

"I found something more," Sune said. "Once I suspected something was very wrong I broke into his computer. It didn't take me long to find out that Christian was the guy that had chatted with Susanne Larsen. He called himself Troels and planned to meet with her at the inn. I also found e-mails from Home Care, you know the company working for the state that assists elderly and disabled people in their homes. Apparently Christian had gotten a job there and went by the name of Svend Henriksen. He took care of Fat Linda Nielsen every Sunday for the past five weeks."

"Wow," I exclaimed. "He has been planning this for a long time, then."

"He sure has. I also found e-mails from an escort-agency where he worked as well. They sent him to visit Marianne and Martin Frandsen the day before yesterday, the night Martin Frandsen was killed. They knew him as Asger. The last thing I found in his e-mail was a confirmation of his new membership to the badminton club where Anders Hoejmark was president."

I nodded pensively. "It was probably also him who called the *Express* anonymously to tip them off so it seemed like he worked there. He knew more about the killings than anyone else. That was also how he managed to always be at the scene so quickly and have all the information."

"Of course," Sune said. "But there is something else. I found more. In the police database."

I looked at him. Then I put down my beer on the table. "I guess it won't surprise me."

"He was investigated during the investigation of his sister's death some ten years ago. She was killed in an institution in Northern Zeeland. Lived in a nursing home for the disabled. One day she was found strangled in her room. They suspected the brother but then another patient admitted to having done it in anger and the case was closed."

I got up from the couch and went to a bookshelf. I pulled out two books and took out a pack of cigarettes hidden for emergencies some months ago. I opened it and lit one. The smoke felt soothing. I offered Sune one and he accepted. This was not a moment to think about our health.

"Thanks," I said after a short break.

"For what?"

"For being a jealous guy."

Sune chuckled. "I guess it paid off for once." He smoked the cigarette then killed the rest in a small ashtray I had put out.

"He would have killed me if you hadn't arrived. I saw the madness in his eyes. They were filled with a strange desire to hurt me. It was like he suddenly changed into this monster. His eyes were nothing like they normally are. It was really strange. Kind of destroys one's belief in the good in human kind. My ability to trust people has been seriously hurt."

I killed my cigarette. Sune said nothing. He stared at me. I looked into his eyes. His face was badly bruised. I stroke it gently. He grabbed my hand. Then he kissed it.

"I love you Rebekka," he said. "Do with it what you want. I just needed to tell you."

I pulled my hand away. He looked at me and exhaled.

"I don't know what to do with that right now," I said.

His eyes were disappointed. This wasn't the answer he was hoping for. But it was all I could give right now.

"All I can think of is the safety of my family right now. I don't know how to protect them with him out there."

Sune stroke my hair. "Let's hope the police find him tonight," he said. "Until then you'll need some rest. I'll stay awake and guard you while you sleep."

"What about Tobias?" I asked. "Where is he right now?"

"I had my neighbor stay with him in my apartment. She's an older lady, she loves taking care of him. They have fun together."

I nodded. "That's good."

"Now go upstairs and get some sleep."

My sleep was uneasy and I woke several times screaming, my pillow soaked from sweat. When it was time to get up and get Julie ready for school I was finally sleeping heavily. It was Julie who woke me up.

"Mom. You have to get up now," she said. "You have to help me get dressed with this cast." I sat up and stared at her wrist. I felt a pinch in my heart. I hated that she had been hurt because of me and

## Three, Four ... Better lock your door

my job. She handed me her shirt and I helped her put it on. "It's kind of cool, mom," she said. "None of my friends has ever broken anything. Elvira from my class once sprained her ankle. But I'm the first to ever have a cast on."

I smiled and kissed her forehead. She was trying so hard to make me feel better. She knew I was guilt plagued. She knew me too well.

"That's good sweetie."

I took a quick shower while Julie packed her backpack and then we went downstairs. The smell of breakfast and coffee filled me with a calmness that everything at least seemed normal. When we entered the kitchen Sune was sitting at the table drinking coffee and eating buttered toast.

"Look who I found in our living room when I came down this morning," Dad said with a smile.

Julie's eyes lit up. I guess mine did too.

"Sune!!" She yelled then ran towards him and hugged him. He kissed her forehead. "What are you doing here? Where's Tobias?" she asked.

"Mrs. Svendsen my neighbor has promised to bring him to school today," he said. Then he looked up at me and smiled. "I had promised your Mom to stay here for the night."

"Why?" Julie asked.

"Enough with all those questions," I said and served her some buttered bread and orange juice. "Eat your breakfast. We're in a hurry."

Sune got up from his chair. "I'd better get back and take a shower as well," he said.

"Get some sleep," I said. "You need it. You can come in later to the office. Maybe bring us all some lunch?"

Sune smiled. "Sounds like a plan," he said just before he left the house.

"Do you care to tell us what is going on?" Dad asked after Julie was done eating and had run upstairs to go to the bathroom before we left. "Sune told me he was here to protect us? That he had promised to stay so you could sleep and not worry? Should I be worried?"

I sighed. "I don't know Dad. To be honest I'm a little confused right now. With Julie getting hurt and yesterday ..." I looked at Dad and realized I was causing him too much worry. I had to spare him and his weak heart. "Well Sune helped me out of a difficult situation."

"You mean he saved you," he said. He shook his head. "Just promise to be careful."

Julie came down the stairs and took on her jacket. "I will, Dad. I promise," I said and followed her out the door.

157

At the office I called Johannes Lindstroem but they hadn't caught Christian Lonstedt yet, he said. He was wanted all over the country and he was sure they would catch him eventually.

"All criminals make mistakes at some point and then we catch them," he said with his calm voice.

I told him I certainly hoped so and hung up. Then I called an old friend of mine. James Wickham. He was a profiling expert for the FBI and an expert in serial killers. I needed to understand and I knew he was the only one who could explain Christian to me.

"Rebekka!" he exclaimed.

"Hi James. How are things?"

"Wonderful. Never been better. Busy though with the kids and everything. Janice is pregnant again so we have enough on our plate. How about you? It's been a couple of years since I last heard from you. Shame on you."

"I've been busy as well. We have another serial killer on our hands," I said.

"Again? What is it this time? More rich men?"

"No this time it's different." I looked through my notes and found the page where I had compared all the victims. "The victims are both male and female. They're very average people, all killed in the shower, the killer has performed lobotomies on all of them with a scalpel - while they were still alive and aware," I said.

"Urgh," he said.

"I know. It's nasty. What can you tell me about him?"

"I'd go after the lobotomies. It's highly unusual. Why would he choose that exact method? Find that and you have the reason why he is killing."

"That's what I thought. I actually found the killer but he escaped and the police are looking for him. But I wanted to know if you could help explain his behavior to me. It was quite strange."

James Wickham was quiet while I told him everything, all the details about my night with Christian and his sudden change in character.

"He kept referring to himself as Victoria," I said. "He acted like he was in fact his sister and Christian was a completely different person."

"Which he probably is when he acts as her," James said.

"What do you mean?"

"It sounds like your friend has invented a superior self to perform his deeds, his killings. He becomes her when he goes out to kill. Is she dead? Is his sister dead?"

"Yes! As a matter of fact she is. He told me that he was sort of revenging her death. That she had asked him to."

## Three, Four ... Better lock your door

"That makes sense. See he has sort of recreated her in his mind. She is alive in his fractured psyche. They must have been close. How was the relationship to their parents?"

"According to Victoria she killed them. First she asked Christian to do it, but he couldn't so she did it herself."

"So she was the dominant one, he was weak and her puppet while growing up. And he was probably a constant source of disappointment, which he still is in his mind, in his recreation of their relationship. He has brought her back because he needs her. He can only kill when he thinks he is her. He has brought her back in his mind and given her new life and maybe even a higher level of cruelty than when she was living. When he is his sister he acts, talks and dresses as she did or would do. He has developed a split personality in which he is two persons. And he can switch between them whenever necessary. He doesn't need to be dressed up. When he is the brother he can live guilt free and normally not affected by what he does and thinks when he is the sister. He is also the type who takes delight in his own achievements. He is proud of his killings."

"And the type who shows up to look at the police working at the crime scene?" I asked. "Looking like nothing but a spectator?"

"Oh yes. He would definitely do that."

I noted everything James told me on my notepad while thinking of Christian who had been so nice and sweet to me and in the next second tried to kill me. It gave me the chills.

"So how do we find a guy like this?"

"He - or she - will not stop now. He is too close to the goal, too close to the revenge he has been seeking. The question is what is it he is revenging? Why did he choose those exact victims? I would take a closer look at the sister. How did she die?"

"I think he killed her," I said.

"That makes sense too," James said. "By resurrecting her in his mind he sort of erased the crime of killing her. My guess is that the lobotomy is somehow linked to his sister's death. Find out who she was and you'll find out why he became who he is."

"Will do," I said. "Thank you so much."

"Anytime Rebekka. You know that."

I hung up and stared at my computer screen without even seeing it. An idea was forming in my mind. I got up and found the files I received from Mogens Holst. Sara took off her headset and stared at me while I placed all the folders in small piles on the floor. Then I looked at her.

"I think I might need your help to go through these," I said.

She got up from her chair and waddled towards me. "I think so too," she said and grabbed a file.

## Chapter 40

SUNE BROUGHT US LUNCH AROUND NOON AND CHIPPED IN ON GOING through the files and piles of paper-works from Lundegaarden. We all read through the material in silence. It was truly horrific. It seemed Mogens Holst had been right. Lundegaarden had been a sort of experimental center for criminals who were too young to go to prison and were sentenced to a life in a closed institution. As far as I could figure it was a place where they placed young people they had no idea what to do with. Then they experimented on them. Lobotomy was performed on more than a hundred young people there and every report stated the surgery somehow improved their lives by removing the pain and discomfort they suffered and turning them into apathetic vegetables. The doctors believed that they had somehow helped society and spared them from many years in prison and spared human lives because these young people were nothing but ticking time bombs who would surely explode if they were released into society. This was being done to help society as well as the young people. It was a gain for everybody.

Among the names of patients I found Victoria Lonstedt. She had a lobotomy performed on June 23, 1993. She had been sentenced to a life in custody when she was only nine years old after killing her parents in their beds at night. According to the papers she had tied them to the bed and stabbed them with a kitchen knife while they slept. Then she set the house on fire and helped her brother to get out while she watched her parents go up into flames. She had taken all the blame and told the police that her brother had nothing to do with it. She was placed in one institution after another but got herself in trouble everywhere. Finally they placed her at Lundegaarden

## Three, Four ... Better lock your door

where they were known to take care of difficult troublemakers. After the lobotomy she calmed down and no longer caused any problems. Then she was released to a nursing home in Northern Zeeland.

I leaned back and told Sune and Sara what I had found. They were both shocked.

"So you think that Christian killed her in that home and then he went to get revenge?" Sune asked.

I got up and looked at the whiteboard with all the information about the victims. "Listen to this," I said and pointed. "The first victim, Susanne Larsen was a nurse. She was in Palliative care, helping people recovering from brain tumor."

"Yeah, so?" Sune asked.

"Linda Nielsen commonly referred to as 'Fat Linda' was unemployed and lived on welfare. But before that she was a nurse too. Before the depression that led her to overeat. The last victim Martin Frandsen was a doctor before he retired. Do you see it?"

"So they were all doctors and nurses," Sune said. "But what about Anders Hoejmark? He was the president of the local badminton club."

"Not only," Sara said and got up. She went to her desk and found a notepad. She flipped a couple of pages. "When I researched his background I remember finding a similar story. I just didn't think it was important since it was so far back in time so I didn't put it up there. There is it. Yes. He was also a doctor from 1982-1993. Then he stopped and in 1995 he became president of the badminton club here in Karrebaeksminde."

"So they have all been nurses and doctors," I repeated while walking back to my computer. "Now we need to see if at any point in time they worked at Lundegaarden."

It didn't take long for Sune and Sara to find out that they all worked at Lundegaarden in 1993 when Victoria was lobotomized, and by looking through her file and the report about the procedure, we quickly realized that all four were present in the operating room on June 23, 1993. Dr. Martin Frandsen performed the procedure, while Dr. Anders Hoejmark assisted. Linda Nielsen and Susanne Larsen were the surgical nurses.

"So those were the four who turned Victoria into a vegetable," Sune said. "Now Christian is taking revenging by acting as her, is that it?"

"Sounds like it," I stated.

"So how do we find him?" Sara said.

"We find his next victim," I said and grabbed the report again. I found the paper recommending a lobotomy for Victoria Lonstedt. I scanned the paper and looked at the signature. The doctor who had signed the paper and doomed Victoria to a life of apathy was not unfamiliar to me.

It was Dr. Irene Hoeg.

## Chapter 41

DR. IRENE HOEG WAS AN UNSATISFIED WOMAN. SHE ALWAYS HAD BEEN but now she was more than ever. Things weren't going exactly as planned. She was swearing and cursing as she packed her suitcase. The day's events had made her miserable. Everything was falling apart now. Ever since that nosy journalist from *Zeeland Times* had been at her house and started talking about the procedures they had done back then and mentioned the name of that irritating Mogens Holst, she had known that it was time to act. She tried what she normally always did, she abused her powers.

First she had someone follow the journalist as she visited Holst whom Irene thought she had managed to shut up for good two years ago by discrediting his name in public. Dr. Irene Hoeg knew many people in high positions and once her private investigator had found the papers stating that Mogens Holst was mentally unstable it hadn't taken much persuasion from her to convince people funding him to stop sending him money for his research and his publisher to have him withdraw the book. Plus she had leaked the story of the insane historian and his ridiculous insinuations that was all a hoax to all the media and even threatened the news-director at the national television that she would reveal his dirty secret of screwing the intern if he didn't do it. It had cost Mogens Holst his job and his family but that only goes to show him that you don't mess with Dr. Irene Hoeg.

But apparently he hadn't been scared enough to not let Rebekka Franck leave the place with plenty of information and documentation to write the story.

Irene Hoeg pulled a dress angrily from a hanger in the closet and threw it in the suitcase. It was going to be warm where she was going and she needed only to pack light clothes like dresses and shorts. The rest she would have to leave here. The pictures of Rebekka Franck leaving Mogens Holst's place with her arms filled with files and papers were on the bed next to her. How she cursed them.

"Little nosy annoying bitch," she hissed.

Next thing she had done was to send someone to shut Rebekka Franck up. He had gone straight to her weak spot, her daughter and threatened her. Her guy had even hurt the daughter by scaring the horse and caused her to fall off. Dr. Irene Hoeg didn't agree much with those kinds of methods but as long as it did the job, she was happy.

She wasn't happy now. The private investigator she had following Rebekka Franck and watching her from the building across the street had just called interrupting her lunch with someone important to the cause of her political party. The investigator said Rebekka Franck and her co-workers had opened the files after all and were now reading them.

That was when Dr. Irene Hoeg dropped her fork into the foie gras at the nice restaurant and told the important politician she was meeting with, that she was very sorry but it was time for her to go now.

"An emergency has occurred."

Then she left the restaurant knowing she wouldn't come back. She had to leave the country. This journalist wouldn't be discredited. Irene had tried to find dirt on her but hadn't succeeded yet to her great frustration. Rebekka Franck was someone people believed in. What she wrote was highly respected even if it was just in a small newspaper. All the other newspapers would jump in on the story as well. When the story broke it was certain to create a furor, an outrage about her personality and her past in the media that she didn't need right now. It would hurt the party and the cause they fought for. The Prime minister would be made responsible and she would drag Irene Hoeg with her in the fall. The cause for which she had worked in years would be destroyed and she couldn't have that. Her dreams about a clean Denmark where wrong people with issues that caused them to be criminal or even just a burden to society because of their flawed brains had to be put down for awhile. It had to wait. The Danes weren't ready for it yet. They weren't ready for Irene Hoeg.

She picked up the photos of Rebekka Franck and looked at them one last time before she threw them in the trash where they belonged.

Once she was done packing she would burn down the house. She had a nice place in Mallorca where she would hide for the next few years until things calmed down a little and it was time to come back. She would return, stronger and wiser and with even greater dreams for a great nation. She wasn't going to give up this easily. Dreams were always hard to realize and Irene knew she had to fight for them to make them come true. Maybe it wouldn't even be in her lifetime, but she had her crown-prince in the party that she could pass the torch to. He could run the party while she was gone and into the future, she could control him from her hideout and help him get more power. All the great generals and strategists through history had fought their battles far from the battlefield. She could do that too.

Dr. Irene Hoeg smiled by the thought. It wasn't over yet. The fight was far from lost. They were only experiencing temporary opposition. This was acceptable, nothing but a bump in the road.

Irene Hoeg sighed with a slight satisfaction. Accepting things for what they were was the only way to remain peaceful in a situation like this. So that was exactly what she was going to do. When it all came down to it she was actually looking forward to spending more time on the island of Mallorca in a milder climate where people didn't question her motives or threaten to destroy her.

Yes it was going to be a nice recreation where she could get ready for the second act of her plan undisturbed, Irene thought as she turned on the water in the bathroom. She would take one last shower in this house and then leave it forever.

Hardly had she stepped in and got her hair soaking wet before someone knocked on the front door.

## Chapter 42

Dr. Irene Hoeg pulled the front door open with a very aggressive expression. "What?" she yelled even before she looked at the person standing outside at the doorstep. She was wearing nothing but a bathrobe and a towel around her hair.

She had considered not opening it at all but the person ringing the doorbell had been very persistent and it had quite frankly become too annoying so she had finally given up and walked downstairs ready to give whoever it was quite the scolding of a lifetime. Dr. Irene Hoeg was tired of people interfering with her life and business. People should learn to mind their own business and not disturb decent people when they were trying to get out of this forsaken country where everybody was oh so proud to be caring about each other and no one was forgotten and left out and where poor helpless people could kill someone in a weak moment because they weren't well and then just get away with it because they were too young to be punished or declared mentally ill or psychotic at the moment of action. That was nonsense to Dr. Irene Hoeg. She did believe that some people couldn't help it because they had a defect in the brain, because they weren't wired right, but she also believed in evil. Some people were just cruel and needed to be hidden from the world and sedated or even pacified if necessary. She believed she had the cure for both.

But right now Dr. Irene Hoeg was standing in front of pure evil, and knew there was no way she would escape it.

"That dress," she stuttered.

"Pretty, isn't it?" the person replied.

"I ... I ..." but there were no more words. Irene Hoeg had run out of things to say. "I gave that to her," she mumbled.

"Yes you did," the voice replied.

## Three, Four ... Better lock your door

Irene lifted her head and eyes from the sparkling blue dress and stared into the eyes of the person wearing it. To her disappointment the eyes resembled but didn't belong to the person she had given the dress to. She looked like her but Irene Hoeg knew it wasn't her.

"What do you want? Why are you ringing my doorbell?" she said.

The person in front of her giggled. "Well you locked the door. Normally I would just walk in."

Dr. Irene Hoeg sighed. So many memories came back to her in that instant. So many happy hours she had spent with this girl. She reached out and touched her cheek, stroked it gently. It didn't feel like her skin had felt. It was too rough. Had it only been her, could she just see her one more time, just touch her soft skin and kiss those red lips.

"Victoria ...," she said, her voice trembling from the memories that now overwhelmed her. The emotions were powerful, devastating, crushing. For the first time in twenty years, Dr. Irene Hoeg cried. She felt a tear in the corner of her eye and she didn't stop to wipe it away.

"You know she loved you, didn't you?" the person in the blue dress looking so strikingly like her asked.

Dr. Irene Hoeg nodded. "All she wanted was a pretty dress to wear. She never had one she told me. So I bought this one for her. She looked stunning in it."

"She spent her life in one institution after the other," the person said. "Until you did that to her, until you made her into nothing but a vegetable." The person in the dress was shaking. "Why? Why would you do this to her?"

"I used to bring her to my office. I fell in love with her. She was so beautiful, so perfect. I could hardly believe it. I felt frustrated. I wasn't supposed to be with the youngsters, with my patients but I couldn't help it. I fell in love with her. I had the nurses bring her to my office late in the evening where I had sex with her. I used her. To compensate I gave her special favors at the institution. She was allowed to smoke cigarettes in her room, cigarettes that I gave her. I brought her better food on special days and celebrated her birthday with a nice dinner in my office. I even took her to the beach every now and then under the pretense that I was taking her to see her parent's grave and keep her focused on what she had done. I thought I was giving her a better life, but it was eating me alive."

Dr. Irene Hoeg was crying now. Tears were rolling down her cheeks as she stared at this woman from her past. The only real love she had ever experienced in her long life.

"So why kill who she was? If you loved my sister so much then why would you sign the papers stating that a lobotomy was the best cure for her?"

Irene Hoeg was bent forward in pain, overpowered by emotions she had tried so hard to escape for many years, dirty disgusting emotions that she thought she had under control.

"Because it was destroying me," she mumbled, sobbing, groaning. "My passion for her was destroying me. It made me soft. I have a purpose, a dream and I couldn't have someone like Victoria be in the way of that. I hated myself for signing those papers, but I had to. There was no other way out for me. I was falling for her, but she was dangerous to me. I was going into politics and I couldn't have this kind of dirt in my past." Irene Hoeg paused. Then she looked at the person in front of her, looked him straight in the eyes as she spoke. "But I wasn't the one who killed her. You were."

Dr. Irene Hoeg felt something grab her around the neck and she was pushed backwards into the hall of her own house. She muttered words but nothing but half-choked sounds spluttered out of her. The pain was excruciating but she knew she deserved it.

## Chapter 43

WE CALLED THE POLICE FROM THE CAR. SUNE DROVE WHILE I SPOKE to Johannes Lindstroem and told him about our theory and that I believed that Christian Lonstedt was on his way to kill Dr. Irene Hoeg. If he wasn't already there.

"We'll send someone to check it out," he said. Then he paused. "Please promise me you will stay out of it."

"I'm sorry. No can do," I said as we hit the highway towards Copenhagen and Hellerup north of it where Dr. Irene Hoeg lived in her big villa. I heard Johannes Lindstroem protest wildly as I hung up. Christian was my business now and I had to stop him before he struck again.

I knew how the Danish police worked and it was going to take hours for Johannes Lindstroem to convince the local department in Hellerup to send a patrol to disturb not only one of the most prominent politicians in the country but also the most choleric one. There was so much bureaucracy in the Danish police, so many people who didn't want to make the difficult decisions and therefore postponed it by referring the problem to someone else. There was no way I was going to let Christian get away with another killing. It was bad enough that he had been there all this time, right under my nose without me even suspecting he could be the killer. I shivered at the thought of having sex with him in his apartment, his hands on my body, the same hands that had killed all these people in cold blood.

Sune looked at me while he drove. "Do we have a plan or anything?" he asked.

I shook my head. "To save a life I guess. Even if it is Dr. Irene Hoeg's. Christian needs to be stopped."

"Sounds like enough for me," he said and took the exit towards

Hellerup. We speeded to the extent that Sune would lose his driver's license for life if he were caught. But he didn't and soon we parked the car in front of the house. I was sweating. I suddenly doubted that we knew what we were doing. How were we supposed to do this?

Sune took out a baseball-bat from the trunk of his car and swung it over his shoulder. Then he grabbed my hand and held it for just a second while we walked towards the white villa. He smiled comforting and that really helped.

No one answered when we rang the doorbell. My heart was racing. Had we come too late? The sound of turmoil came from an opened window upstairs. I looked up. Someone was struggling, fighting.

"They're up there," I said and pointed toward the window.

Sune pulled the handle. "It's not locked," he said and pushed the door open. We hurried inside and ran up the stairs. There was a scream, a bump and then silence.

We ran from room to room and found them in the bathroom. Christian was bent over Dr. Irene Hoeg's lifeless body on the floor. He had dropped the wig that was lying on the tiles next to him. Irene Hoeg had closed eyes; her head was bleeding from the back. Christian had the scalpel in his hand, ready to cut when I entered through the open door.

"Stop!" I yelled. "Victoria, stop!"

Christian turned and looked at me. The make-up was smeared all over his face. His eyes wore that cruelty in them that they had the last time I had seen him when he was about to make me his next victim.

When he saw me, he smiled. Then he giggled. "Come any closer and I'll cut her main artery."

I froze. Sune was right behind me. I raised my hand to hold him back. "Is she still alive? he asked.

"I don't know," I answered. My heart was pounding in my chest. There was blood on the floor next to her head, but it looked like she was breathing.

"You both came right in time for the good part," Christian said. "The final act." He stared at Irene Hoeg. Then he stroked her forehead and removed a lock of hair that had fallen down.

"The doctor hurt her head a little bit so she won't be attending the procedure, but I think we can go ahead and do it anyway," he said. "I thought about waiting till she woke up so she could see for herself how it is done, but you kind of ruined that."

"Is it important to you that she is awake?" I asked.

He turned and stared at me. "I prefer it that way. It makes it more fun."

# Three, Four ... Better lock your door

"Did you wake up your parents just before you killed them as well?" I asked.

Christian nodded. "I did it for him, you know. Well for both of us, but mostly for him. He was hurting. I wasn't sure he would be able to survive it."

"You mean your brother, Christian?" I asked.

Christian smiled. "Of course. Who else? He was my only concern. See as I told you he was the weak one. I was strong I could take almost everything without letting it get to me. That was just who I was, but not Christian. He couldn't take the constant abuse."

"Did your parents abuse you?" I asked. "Was that why you killed them?"

Christian looked at me with menace in his eyes. It startled me. I felt Sune's hand on my shoulder.

"It wasn't only them," he said with distant voice. "It was all of their friends even acquaintances, anyone who was willing to pay what they asked. Every day it was someone new, every day new hands, new bodies, wrinkled bodies, old penises, hands touching us all over our bodies, pulling us, holding us down, penetrating us, forcing their sex in our mouths. Every single day of our lives. What really truly hurt was they didn't even charge them much for it." He paused and looked away. "I had to protect him. He wasn't able to do it himself. I had it all planned out and I needed him to help, but he backed out. Said he couldn't do it. I didn't understand after all they had done to us? How could he want to protect them? How come he didn't lust for revenge? How come he didn't want for them to suffer like we had? So I did it myself. I took the blame. Told them Christian had nothing to do with it. At least that way he would get his own life, he would be free to live. I told him to never visit, but he kept coming. He was a good boy, still is. I was the one who ruined everything for him."

"How?"

"I asked him to kill me. After the lobotomy I was nothing but a vegetable. I could hardly move. I sat in a wheelchair every day for years doing nothing but drooling. I hated it; I loathed myself and my helplessness. I was already dead. So when he came to visit I asked him to kill me. I begged him. Slowly over the years I took over his mind and showed him how to do it. I persuaded him like I convinced him to revenge what they had done to me. It is all my doing. Christian could never do it alone." He paused and sighed. "Now I would like to finish what I have begun."

"I can't let you do that," I said.

"Try and stop me," he said. "If you move I'll kill her."

It happened so fast I hardly noticed it. I felt Sune's hand push me backwards, and then from the corner of my eye I saw him swing the baseball-bat in the air and hit Christian in the face so hard he flew across the bathroom and landed on the tiles.

"Wow," I exclaimed. "Where did that come from?"

"I figured that if we moved he would kill her but if we didn't he would still kill her so we had nothing to lose."

I stared at Christian who lay still on the tiles. Blood was coming from where the baseball-bat had hit him. His eyes were closed but he was breathing. I exhaled. In the distance I heard sirens wailing.

## Chapter 44

WE STAYED AND MADE OUR STATEMENTS TO THE POLICE AND SEVERAL hours later we were in the car on our way back to Karrebaeksminde. Neither of us spoke much since we had spent the last hours explaining and talking to police officers. Explaining the entire case and the chain of events to them. Now we felt exhausted and all we wanted was to go home to our children. My dad had picked both of the kids up from school and brought them back to his house where they were now sound asleep on the couch as we entered the house. We carried them upstairs and put them in Julie's room. Then we walked down to the kitchen. Dad said goodnight and I found a bottle of wine that I opened and poured some into two glasses.

I lifted my glass and looked into Sune's eyes.

"Thank you," I said.

"Thank yourself. You solved the case."

"Couldn't have done it alone," I said and drank.

"True," he said.

I found my cell phone and called a number.

"This better be good, Franck," Jens-Ole said. "I just made popcorn and started the movie."

"I think you'll see that this is worth losing a few minutes of your movie for."

He paused. Sune smiled. "I'm listening."

"I have two stories for you. First one is that they have caught the lobotomy killer. The second is linked to the first story. You better sit down for it."

"I'm perfectly fine where I am," he said. "Bring it on."

I told Jens-Ole everything. All about Lundegaarden, the Prime

Minister, Dr. Irene Hoeg, the lobotomy killer's connection and Mogens Holst. When I was done, he went quiet.

"You were right," he said. "I had to sit down while you were talking." Then he paused again. "Why the hell haven't I heard anything about this story until now?" He said.

"Well you told me it wasn't worth looking into as far as I recall. 'A waste of time,' I think you called it," I said.

"Well I guess I was wrong," he said. "Do you realize what this means? This could overthrow the government!"

"I know. So what do you say?"

"I say write this thing, write till your fingers bleed. But take your time. This needs to be well documented and well-researched. No one should be able to put a finger on this story afterwards and tell us we didn't do our job well enough. Cause they will try. Be certain of that. They will try to discredit you and your work. Don't give them the possibility to do that. First write the story about the lobotomy killer. Then we will run the next story big time in the coming days, even better weeks. Let's overthrow that government!"

"Let's do that. Now get back to your movie," I said and hung up.

I sighed with relief. Sune stared at me. "Are you sure about this?" He asked. "It was quite a scare you had the other day with Julie. What if they try something again?"

I exhaled and drank. Then I put my glass on the table. "I think I would be more scared if I chose not to do this," I said. "Scared of who I was becoming and where this country was going."

Our eyes locked. I felt a thrill inside from being with him again like this. Then I leaned over and pressed my lips against his. He pushed me away.

"Are you sure about that?" he asked.

I shook my head. "No."

His eyes looked disappointed. I leaned over and grabbed his shirt. I pulled him close. So close our lips almost touched. I felt his breath on my face.

"But I am sure I want to do it anyway," I said.

Then we kissed again.

## THE END
### Want to know what happens next?
Get the third book in the Rebekka Franck series here :
***Five, Six ... Grab your Crucifix***

# Afterword

**Dear reader,**

Thank you for purchasing *Three, Four ... Better lock your door* (Rebekka Frank #2).

I hope you enjoyed reading it as much as I did writing it. If you liked the settings and the creepy parts, then you might as well enjoy the series of scary short-stories that I released earlier: HORROR STORIES FROM DENMARK. They all take place in Rebekka Franck's hometown and are related to this series. You can get them and my other books and series below.

You can also read an excerpt from my newly released mystery novel *Itsy Bitsy Spider*, the first in my Emma Frost-series on the following pages.

If you could leave a honest review of this book then that would make me very happy .

Take care,
Willow Rose

**Connect with Willow online and you will be the first to know about new releases and bargains from Willow Rose**
*Sign up to the VIP email here:*
http://readerlinks.com/l/415254
I promise not to share your email with anyone else, and I won't clutter your inbox. I'll only contact you when a new book is out or when I have a special bargain/free eBook.

Follow Willow Rose on BookBub:
https://www.bookbub.com/authors/willow-rose

# Books by the Author

**Mystery/Horror Novels:**

- What Hurts the Host (7th Street Crew #1) - Grab your copy today
- You Can Run (7th Street Crew #2) - Grab your copy today
- You Can't Hide (7th Street Crew #3) - Grab your copy today
- Carefull Little Eyes (7th Street Crew #4) - Grab your copy today

- Hit the Road Jack (Jack Ryder #1) - Grab your copy today
- Slip Out the Back Jack (Jack Ryder #2) - Grab your copy today
- The House that Jack Built (Jack Ryder #3) - Grab your copy today
- Black Jack (Jack Ryder #4) - Grab your copy today
- Girl next door (Jack Ryder #5) - Grab your copy today
- Her final word (Jack Ryder #6) - Grab your copy today

- One, Two... He is Coming for You (Rebekka Franck #1) - Grab your copy today
- Three, Four ... Better Lock your Door (Rebekka Franck #2) - Grab your copy today
- Five, Six ... Grab your Crucifix (Rebekka Franck #3) - Grab your copy today
- Seven, Eight... Gonna Stay up Late (Rebekka Franck #4) - Grab your copy today
- Nine, Ten... Never Sleep Again (Rebekka Franck #5) - Grab your copy today
- Eleven, Twelve... Dig and Delve (Rebekka Franck #6) - Grab your copy today
- Thirteen, Fourteen... Little Boy Unseen (Rebekka Franck #7) - Grab your copy today
- Better not cry (Rebekka Franck #8) - Grab your copy today
- Ten little Girls (Rebekka Franck #9) - Grab your copy today

- EDWINA - Grab your copy today
- TO HELL IN A HANDBASKET - Grab your copy today
- UMBRELLA MAN - Grab your copy today
- BLACK BIRD FLY - Grab your copy today

- ITSY BITSY SPIDER (Emma Frost #1) - Grab your copy today
- MISS POLLY HAD A DOLLY (Emma Frost #2)- Grab your copy today
- RUN, RUN, AS FAST AS YOU CAN (Emma Frost #3) - Grab your copy today
- CROSS YOUR HEART AND HOPE TO DIE (Emma Frost #4) - Grab your copy today
- PEEK A BOO I SEE YOU (Emma Frost #5) - Grab your copy today
- TWEEDLEDUM AND TWEEDLEDEE (Emma Frost #6) - Grab your copy today
- EASY AS ONE TWO THREE (Emma Frost #7) - Grab your copy today
- THERE'S NO PLACE LIKE HOME (Emma Frost #8) - Grab your copy today
- SLENDERMAN (Emma Frost #9) - Grab your copy today
- WHERE THE WILD ROSES GROW (Emma Frost #10) - Grab your copy today
- WALTZING MATHILDA (Emma Frost #11) - Grab your copy today
- DRIP DROP DEAD (Emma Frost #12) - Grab your copy today

**Horror Short Stories:**

- EENIE, MEENIE - Grab your copy today
- ROCK-A-BYE BABY - Grab your copy today
- NIBBLE, NIBBLE, CRUNCH - Grab your copy today
- HUMPTY, DUMPTY - Grab your copy today
- CHAIN LETTER - Grab your copy today
- BETTER WATCH OUT - Grab your copy today
- MOMMY DEAREST - Grab your copy today
- THE BIRD - Grab your copy today

**Paranormal Romance/Suspense/Fantasy Novels:**

- FLESH AND BLOOD - Grab your copy today
- BLOOD AND FIRE - Grab your copy today
- FIRE AND BEAUTY - Grab your copy today
- BEAUTY AND BEASTS - Grab your copy today
- BEASTS AND MAGIC - Grab your copy today
- MAGIC AND WITCHCRAFT - Grab your copy today
- WITCHCRAFT AND WAR - Grab your copy today
- WAR AND ORDER - Grab your copy today
- ORDER AND CHAOS- Grab your copy today
- CHAOS AND COURAGE - Grab your copy today

---

- THE SURGE - Grab your copy today
- GIRL DIVIDED - Grab your copy today
- BEYOND (Afterlife #1) - Grab your copy today
- SERENITY (Afterlife #2) - Grab your copy today
- ENDURANCE (Afterlife #3) - Grab your copy today
- COURAGEOUS (Afterlife #4) - Grab your copy today
- SAVAGE (Daughters of the Jaguar #1) - Grab your copy today
- BROKEN (Daughters of the Jaguar #2) - Grab your copy today
- SONG FOR A GYPSY (The Eye of the Crystal Ball -The Wolfboy Chronicles) - Grab your copy today
- I AM WOLF (The Wolfboy Chronicles) - Grab your copy today

---

**Box Sets:**

- JACK RYDER MYSTERY SERIES BOX SET: VOL 1-3 - Grab your copy today
- REBEKKA FRANCK SERIES VOL 1-3 - Grab your copy today
- REBEKKA FRANCK SERIES VOL 4-6 - Grab your copy today
- REBEKKA FRANCK SERIES VOL 1-5 - Grab your copy today
- EMMA FROST MYSTERY SERIES VOL 1-3 - Grab your copy today
- EMMA FROST MYSTERY SERIES VOL 4-6 - Grab your copy today
- EMMA FROST MYSTERY SERIES VOL 7-9 - Grab your copy

today
- EMMA FROST MYSTERY SERIES VOL 1-5 - Grab your copy today
- DAUGHTERS OF THE JAGUAR BOX SET - Grab your copy today
- THE VAMPIRES OF SHADOW HILLS: BOOKS 1-3 - Grab your copy today
- THE AFTERLIFE SERIES (BOOKS 1-3)- Grab your copy today
- HORROR STORIES FROM DENMARK - Grab your copy today
- THE WOLFBOY CHRONICLES - Grab your copy today

## About the Author

The Queen of Scream aka Willow Rose is a #1 Amazon Best-selling Author and an Amazon ALL-star Author of more than 50 novels. She writes Mystery, Paranormal, Romance, Suspense, Horror, Supernatural thrillers, and Fantasy.

Willow's books are fast-paced, nail-biting page-turners with twists you won't see coming.

Several of her books have reached the Kindle top 20 of ALL books in the US, UK, and Canada.

She has sold more than three million books.

Willow lives on Florida's Space Coast with her husband and two daughters. When she is not writing or reading, you will find her surfing and watch the dolphins play in the waves of the Atlantic Ocean.

**To be the first to hear about new releases and bargains from Willow Rose. Sign up to be on the VIP list below.**

I promise not to share your email with anyone else, and I won't clutter your inbox.

http://readerlinks.com/l/415254

**Tired of too many emails?** Text the word: "willowrose" to 31996 to sign up to Willow's VIP text List to get a text alert with news about New Releases, Giveaways, Bargains and Free books from Willow.

FOLLOW WILLOW ROSE ON BOOKBUB:
https://www.bookbub.com/authors/willow-rose

***Connect with Willow online:***
https://www.facebook.com/willowredrose
www.willow-rose.net
http://www.goodreads.com/author/show/ 4804769.Willow_Rose
https://twitter.com/madamwillowrose
madamewillowrose@gmail.com

- facebook.com/willowredrose
- twitter.com/madamwillowrose
- instagram.com/madamewillowrose

Printed in Great Britain
by Amazon